A Publisher's Note

To my dearest readers:

Triple Crown Publications provides you with the best reads in hip-hop fiction. Each novel is hand-selected in its purest form with you, the reader, in mind. *Let That Be the Reason*, an insta-classic, pioneered the hip-hop genre. Always innovative, you can count on Triple Crown's growth: manuscript notes — published books — audio — film.

Triple Crown has also gone international, with novels distributed around the globe. In Tokyo, the books have been translated into Japanese. Triple Crown's revolutionary brand has garnered attention from prominent news media, with features in ABC News, The New York Times, Newsweek, MTV, Publisher's Weekly, The Boston Globe, Vibe, Essence, Entrepreneur Magazine, Inc Magazine, Black Enterprise Magazine, The Washington Post, Millionaire Blueprints Magazine and Writer's Digest, just to name a few. I recently earned Ball State University's Ascent Award for Entrepreneurial Business Excellence and was named by Book Magazine as one of publishing's 50 most influential women. Those prestigious honors have taken me from street corner to boardroom accreditation.

Undisputedly, Triple Crown is the leader of the urban fiction renaissance, boasting more than one million sizzling books sold and counting...

Without you, our readers, there is no us,

Vickie Stringer
Publisher

Trickery

BY CHRISTINE RACHEAL

Compilation and Introduction copyright © 2010 by
Triple Crown Publications
PO Box 247378
Columbus, Ohio 43224
www.TripleCrownPublications.com

Library of Congress Control Number: 2009940700
ISBN 13: 978-0-9825888-9-5

Author: Christine Racheal
Graphics Design: Valerie Thompson, Leap Graphics
Photography: Treagen Kier
Editor-in-Chief: Vickie Stringer
Editor: Christina Carter
Editorial Assistant: Matthew Allan Roberson

First Trade Paperback Edition Printing 2010

10 9 8 7 6 5 4 3 2 1

Printed in the United States of America

Acknowledgements

First, the deepest, most heart-felt thank-you goes to God for being my everything and for blessing me with life and creativity. (I could go on all day).

A special thanks to my support system, my family, who has been there, sacrificed for me, and kept me lifted in prayer. I thank God for you all. I love you.

Thank you, Vickie Stringer, for calling out my talent and taking a chance on me.

To those who inspired me to write this book, those who have been behind me through the course of this project, and to the "I Can Make It Happen" crew (you know who you are), thank you.

And to my readers: thank you, thank you, thank you.

God Bless You All.

Dedication

To those taking refuge in darkness,
I've found light to be so liberating.
Solutions are never within, but above.

Chapter One

She was naked before I poured my first drink. The towel was draped loosely around her petite 5-foot-3, 110-pound frame. She danced slowly in the mirror at the headboard, over the bed laced with sticky sheets. She kneeled there, touching her body seductively. The thick, cool air from the window unit blasted at her body, causing her hair to blow in its heavy current. I pretended not to watch her reflection from the mirror above the dresser.

"You think they'll find the place this time?" I asked, face buried in a glass of vodka with no chaser.

"I hope so. The Madison Inn is a good location. Two of 'em already called my phone lookin' for the spot, so they should be on the way," she replied, hips moving to the rhythm of some stripper anthem playing on the CD player.

Everyone called her Tiki. No one cared to know her real name, not even me. She was a mix breed, the sexy results of a black and Asian unprotected sexual encounter. She offered no other information. I met her through a friend, and all I needed to know was that she was about her business and didn't keep up with any drama. I needed her on my team.

The raggedy hotel room smelled like damp, soured carpet

and stale cigarettes, an upgrade from the roach-infested hotel we occupied the night before. Both the microwave and the fridge smelled like animal carcass and held remnants of meals from previous occupants. It was hard to breathe. Tiki walked into the bathroom, and I pulled the top comforter from the bed and threw it onto the floor. I heard somewhere that hotel staff less frequently wash comforters than sheets, and I imagined the men and women who had soaked the dressings with their internal-turned-external bodily fluids and it almost made me vomit.

"What are you doing, Taj?" she walked into the room, pulling her thick black hair up from her shoulders into a ponytail.

"I'm getting ready."

"By taking off the covers?" She lifted the comforter from the floor.

"I'll do it my way. Trust me. It's better than catching a case of crabs."

She walked back into the bathroom. I picked up my duffle bag full of toiletries and followed her in.

"So, what are you wearing tonight?" she asked.

"Something I snatched from Vicky's. I just hope it fits."

"It don't matter. You'll be coming out of it soon." Her lips formed the most attractive smirk I had ever seen.

There was a knock. We both looked at each other, suggesting that one of us goes to check it out.

"Why don't you go, Tiki, and I'll jump in a quick shower. Please."

"All right, chick. Make it quick. Showtime in fifteen."

"Gotcha."

It seemed like I couldn't get clean enough. One layer of dirt and oil removed from my skin, another one added from showering in such a filthy space. The miniature bar of soap broke into pieces in my washcloth. I removed the largest chunk and slid it across my body: the breasts, the thighs, my neck, between my fingers and toes, between my legs. Sweat, induced by liquor and a heated shower, beaded on my forehead and was rinsed away, careful not to wet my hair. Then, someone walked into the bathroom. My heart sank into my stomach.

"Tiki?"

"Nah, shawty, you straight. I just gotta piss real quick." I peeped from behind the shower curtain. He unzipped his jeans, stitched with the True Religion emblem on the back pocket, a

2

Trickery

good indication that he had money to spend.

"And your name is?" I asked with an attitude, offended that he would enter without knocking.

"It's Terrance."

"Ok. I'm Taj. Make yourself comfortable. I'll be out in a minute." I played nicely.

"All right. All right." He walked out and closed the door behind himself. Although he didn't wash his hands, I was glad he wasn't one that had to be forced out.

I tiptoed around the dirty, wet towel Tiki had laid on the floor that now held several of Terrance's filthy footprints. Lotion and body oil were applied from shoulders to toes. The tags on the new, red lace Vicky bra and panty set were snapped off; I put them on. I let my hair down. Every silky, black strand lay properly in place. I puckered up for a glossy finish then slid on my black, 4-inch pumps and was ready to begin.

The room had low visibility, fogged by clouds of smoke emitted from the weed-smokers who surrounded the bed in their seats. Three guests stood by the dresser, each of them already refilling their half-empty glass of liquor. All eyes were on me. Tiki was nowhere in sight.

Trickery

"Fellas, ya'll seen Tiki?"

"She went to the lobby for a minute. She'll be right back," Terrance offered.

Just then, she walked into the room with two more men, bringing the total to twelve. They were extremely tall and more handsome than I expected of any of the men there.

"Where you find them?"

"Wandering – looking for a good party."

"A hundred dollars a head, right fellas?"

"We got you, sexy. Damn! It looks worth it to me." He licked his lips then pressed them together. "What you think, Mike?"

"You ain't even gotta ask, man. You know I'm down."

"Mike, huh." I leaned over to touch him, shoulder to shoulder. "You ready?"

"Let's do this." His cap cast a shadow over his eyes and the light put emphasis on his smile, straight white teeth and extremely plump lips.

"Umph!" I flirted. "Smile again."

He blushed a bit, lowering his head and fidgeting his cap. He smiled.

I reached behind myself and hit the switch to turn off the main light in the room. Tiki pressed pause on the stereo for our announcements. All eyes were on us as we walked over to the bed and both kneeled in its center, with our legs gapped open, forming a V shape, teasing them.

"Ok guys, to stay I need your ID. If you don't have a form of ID, I'm sorry but you gotta go." The men reached into their pockets. Most pulled from wallets, others from their hats or socks. Tiki collected each one, stacked them, and placed them in the envelope behind the bed. "If you've been here before, you know the rules." A few gasped, others sighed. "No weapons, no fighting, no touching."

"Well, that is, no touching us," Tiki interjected.

"If you feel like you cannot abide by these terms, leave now. And if you can," I placed my index finger in my mouth and seductively removed it, "the price of admission is a hundred dollars." They reached into their pockets again, many of them without taking their eyes from me.

Tiki collected the money, and then added, "One last thing. This is what I call your lifeline." She held her cell phone in the air and the light illuminated the darkest areas.

Trickery

"At midnight I will make a phone call. If for some reason that phone call is not received, the police will be here before you can think to run," I finished her statement. The men spoke amongst each other. "Also, I only have to press one button to reach the authorities. Don't try anything slick."

Up to that point there had not been any need to phone the local authorities. We had never rehearsed an escape route in the event that something went wrong; and we hoped that no one would give us a reason to do so.

"With that said, let's begin." Tiki pressed play on the CD player and climbed into bed with me.

We began with some kissing, then touching until all of our clothes were removed. She unfastened my 34D Vicky bra with her mouth as she cupped and massaged my breasts with both of her hands. We took turns touching and rubbing and licking each other until an hour had passed. No one left the room, but we were too busy entertaining that we wouldn't have noticed if all of them were gone.

This served as our occupation. The way we made our money was quick and easy. I had been doing shows for almost a year when I met Tiki. Before her, I would perform with various friends who just needed some quick cash to get by for a while, but I needed someone more dependable – someone who needed this life, this profession, as much as I did. Tiki was not only good at entertaining; she was professional. I never had to call and ask if we were still on for a show, if she would be ready on time, or even if she needed a ride. If she said she would be there, she was there.

The money was a different issue. It may have seemed like a lot of money to many, but once three thousand dollars has slid through your fingers for one weekend's work, six hundred dollars a night during the week is only pocket change and is spent as such. We became addicted to it, like some of the drugs we used on a regular basis to escape the reality of what we were doing and the idea of exposing ourselves to so many.

We heard, after a show in Orlando, that a particular pastor had been present. I can't say that I recall how he looked. They all look the same in the dark, when lights are striking my body from every angle. That was our thing: darkness. Who knew what could be found lurking in the night, in hotel rooms, and how a daylight façade dramatically contrasted to a nightly one. I lived for the night; by day I was insignificant.

Trickery

We never dwelled on what people thought of us. It would only hinder us from getting more money. Everybody got their place in life, Tiki would say. And this is ours, I would finish – some ho quote we felt proud to believe we'd made up. We were both eager to have money, and what many considered to be the finer things, but she and I were different. Making money was her main priority, but it kept her from enjoying what piece of life existed for us. On the other hand, I loved to read, to educate myself, even through others. I thought I was as smart as they come, with a sexiness to match. No one could have told me differently.

There was a time that I considered exotic dancing, a seemingly far more acceptable way of making money than engaging in sexual acts with women in hotel rooms. I considered the mediocre pay that I would take home at the end of every night, allowing men to touch me in order to make only a dollar more than the other dancers and having to tip the DJ and bouncers for their services from my hard-earned cash. There were no second thoughts. Entrepreneurship was more attractive. Once, I even considered expanding the business, but that never went anywhere. The performers were so undependable, so I stuck to what I knew, what worked – and that was the Tiki and Taj duo. Tiki was loyal, but I never let my guard down. She was human, was most definitely not me, and so could not be trusted. If she was anything like me, she looked out for herself first, then others second. That's what it took for us to make it.

Trickery

Chapter Two

I spent every Saturday at a bookstore near my apartment in Jacksonville, Florida. There was something about the atmosphere that made me feel rich, better than I was. I picked through the African American fiction section most days, always wondering what elements made it African American fiction: the author or its content. Other times I could be caught thumbing through men's magazines with the hottest female models on the covers. I once submitted photos to numerous male magazines. I received only one callback – for a topless shoot. I declined the offer, even the free trip to New York.

Well-traveled by the age of 21, I had been to numerous major cities in the US, sometimes for play, but primarily for business. Some rapper wants a good show in Atlanta, I'd go. A well-paid athlete looking for entertainment after a victory in Houston, I'm there. Some poor soul is jumping the broom, I may consider. I lived my life for adventure that I couldn't find in the shows alone but the places they took me.

To the naked eye, it appeared that I had everything. It took further examination to realize that it was the total opposite. I was a wreck. No one was allowed in my apartment. I hid a piece of myself there. It was typically dark. Rooms were lit by burning candles or by opening the heavy, dark curtains that kept out most sunlight. My place was barely furnished, having only a loveseat and an end table with a 27-inch television on top. I was rarely there, so I kept my fridge on empty to prevent food from spoiling. There were no rats or roaches, only walls covered with spots from water damage caused by poor plumbing. The one bedroom in the apartment was always a mess. I simply threw costumes from shows in there without hanging or folding anything; fish net stockings sprawled across the floor – red, patent leather boots were at the head of the queen-size bed covered with clothing and costume jewelry. I kept every other space neat, clean.

Three nights after the show at the Madison Inn, I received a phone call from an extremely friendly voice.

"You know I been thinking 'bout you," he said when I answered the phone. I was in my apartment, changing my fingernail polish for that night's show.

"Oh really? And why is that?" I responded.

"I never forget the sexy ones."

"So, I'm sexy now? Okay. Now tell me, who is this?"

"Ah, damn. See."

"Wait, you called me, right?"

"Yeah, this Mike."

"Mike who?" I paused for a moment to make it seem more convincing that I had no clue who he was. It didn't work.

"I can hear you smiling," he said while I chuckled on the other end. "Been waiting for my call, huh?"

"Ew, don't get arrogant now." I wanted to say yes, but it seemed like a cry of desperation. I wasn't waiting for his call, but I expected it, if that makes any sense at all.

"What you doin' tonight?"

"You, if you're nice." I responded, making it his turn to chuckle into the receiver. "I'm kidding. I'm working tonight."

"Oh, and I wasn't invited?"

"Got a hundred dollars?" I was serious.

"So, you'll charge me again?"

"This is business, Mike. You gotta pay to play." There was an awkward silence, like I was awaiting some form of rebuttal. "Well, tomorrow is a good time to get together. Is that cool with you?"

"Yeah. What time?" He didn't hesitate.

"I'll call you." I hung up quickly.

There was something about men and relationships and women and sex that never meshed well together, so I always kept them separate. The security that men provided was overpowered by nights between the sheets with women. And although I tried to find a happy medium, I was never successful. True, lesbian women turned their noses up at the thought of me being bi-sexual. And men embraced the fact that I loved women a little too much, hoping it would lead to threesome activity. Other men became jealous at the thought that I could have possibly slept with more women than they had, or perhaps it was the fact that I was paid to do it on most occasions. For a while I abstained from relationships with either sex. It made life more complicated than it had to be.

Although I didn't reside in the nicest neighborhood, I always kept a nice ride – most of them rented, some borrowed from people who owed me favors. I hated contracts and I never saved enough to pay cash for something I really wanted. As long as I could rent a premium automobile for weeks at a time, I was satisfied: BMW this week, Mercedes next. Stepping out of the sexiest automobiles in Gucci and Prada added to the flair. I became a walking advertisement for both potential clients and partners who admired me. I was always looking for some fresh, young entertainer with a let's-go-get-'em attitude to help increase revenue.

Trickery

The show the night of Mike's phone call went well. I managed to pull in eight hundred dollars in seats and another two hundred in tips, and would have made more had it not been for Tiki's eagerness to go to church the next morning. I never understood why the most troubled sinners sought God after their wrongful acts. I figured I would find time to go to church when I felt as though I was ready to change my ways or if some miraculous blessing would be waiting for me within the sanctuary on a particular Sunday. I knew that God was there somewhere, but for the most part I was alone fighting my own battles.

Mike called me several times on Sunday, more than I could stand. My morning was going slowly. The intoxication from the night before had just begun to wear off.

"Hello?" I answered with a cracking voice.

"You don't sound ready to me."

"That's because I'm not, Mike."

"Well, excuse me for not thinking you'll be awake at three." He paused, and noticed that I didn't respond to his comment. "I was just out and about, and wanted to see if you were hungry. My treat and I can bring it to you."

"This isn't about you bringing me something to eat. You trying to get over here," I sighed heavily, "well, the answer is, no."

"What happened to us seeing each other?"

"We will, when I call you." He was speaking as I hung up.

It wasn't in me to be concerned about the feelings of people who only wanted something from me. Mike wouldn't have cared if I had hung up in his face 10 times that day, as long as he felt there was a possibility that I would be spreading my legs at the end of the night.

I rolled out of bed around five and dressed quickly, afraid that I would completely lose the day's sun. I put on my black lace bra and panty set, and covered up with a red, A-line Marciano dress. I was dehydrated, but I understood that water would elevate the sensation of ecstasy throughout my body. Instead, I unwrapped a sweet piece of gum and chewed until my saliva became satisfying.

"I'm ready now," I said once Mike answered. I sat on the edge of the bed, cluttered with clothing.

Trickery

"Can I come get you?" he said anxiously.

"Not happening. I'll meet you at Regency."

"The mall? Why?"

"Um, because," I stalled, trying to think of some reason he couldn't pick me up, "I have something to pick up today before they close, and since everything is around there, maybe we can get dinner or something."

"What time?"

"Now," I reached down to fasten my shoes. "Is that a problem?"

"No, I'm on the way." He hung up, trying to reciprocate my phone etiquette.

I pretended to have interests in the camera store at the mall in order to follow through with my lie. When he asked what I needed from there, I simply responded that it was no business of his. Dinner was boring. I hate inauthentic Italian food and the conversation consisted of his curiosity about my life in the business, how genius it is, and ideas that may help in future shows. Audio off, I thought to myself. At some point, he even offered a critique of the performance itself, and then offered to be security at the next show – for a fee, of course.

"So, what about us?" I cut off his never-ending monologue. He looked confused. "What do you want from me?"

"I want to know you." He cut an edge of lasagna with his fork and lifted it to his mouth, cheese stretched from the plate. Then I noticed the dimple in his cheek and smirked.

"What part of me? I know you're not here because of my personality," he sat back in his seat, still chewing the last bite. "And everything in me is saying that you got a girl," he looked directly into my eyes. "So, tell me. What do you want?"

"You ready?" He wiped his mouth with the napkin, still chewing.

"Yeah, I'm ready."

He dropped a hundred dollar bill on the table for our waitress, and snatched his keys from the seat beside him. He held my hand as we made our way towards the door, as if it would make me more comfortable. I watched my car fade into the distance through the passenger window of his Hummer as we left the area. We headed toward the beaches, in silence for the most part.

After an awkward, 20-minute ride, we pulled up to his house. You could see the waves crashing on the beach in his backyard. It was exotic. The breeze caused the palm trees lining the driveway to sway and each light flickered on as we pulled closer to the house. We entered the garage and it closed automatically behind us. Mike exited the car and walked around to open my car door. Although he appeared nervous, the situation seemed almost routine to him.

11

Trickery

The inside of his house was far from a bachelor pad. It had a woman's touch. Better yet, it held a woman's presence. Jasmine and lilac oil diffusers created an aromatic atmosphere. As far as I could see, the house had six bedrooms, two living room areas, a dining room and an office in its farthest corner. All of the areas were dark, and I could only glance quickly as Mike escorted me to one of the bedrooms. Once inside, I realized that it couldn't have been the master suite. It was fairly small and held only a queen size bed, a night stand, and a bookshelf near the window. The comforter and curtains were floral print and the room smelled like new carpet, having little to no traffic.

"At least you have the decency to use the guest room." I sat on the bed and began to take off my shoes.

"Don't be rude, Taj." He took off one of his diamond-encrusted chains.

I was cautious, not wanting to ruin the moment.

I undressed quickly and lay across the bed with my head resting on my hands. I watched him, anxiously stumbling with his belt buckle. "What you lookin' at?"

"It's more like what I'm trying to look at. It's taking you long enough." I propped up in bed.

"I guess you would be use to quick niggas."

"And what you mean by that?" I asked, offended that he thought he knew anything about me.

"Never mind," he replied, obviously not trying to ruin the moment either.

He lay in bed, parallel to me, with his arms extended above his head. That was my cue to initiate the activity. I always thought that men felt less guilty about sex if a woman initiated it.

I climbed on top and tugged at his boxers. "You gonna take these off or are we just holding each other and going to sleep?"

He laid there for a moment; seemingly annoyed and trying to psyche himself up to go that far. I placed my chest against his then moved slowly towards his abdomen, leaving tracks with red splotches of lipstick. In no time, I was able to make out each vein of his penis with my tongue. Mike lifted my 5-foot-5, 120-pound body to a position where we were face-to-face, my body on top of his. He kissed me, and in the same motion, used his body weight to turn me over onto my back and pin me. I felt his penis between my legs, close to its target area. I felt him inching closer and closer. I pressed my palm against his chest to alert him that he was moving too far, too fast.

"What you pushin' me for?" He didn't stop sucking at my neck. "Damn, you smell so good."

"Wait." I pushed against him. "Do you have a condom?"

"Yeah, it's in my pocket. My pants are on the floor"

"Well, don't' you think we need it now?" I stopped pushing him. His penis was at the entry way and with the slightest motion he would be completely submerged. He backed away instead. A string of my juices extended about a foot, connected to him, before it became a cold mess on my thigh. He went to his pant pocket and removed the gold Magnum wrapper, which his size definitely did not warrant. Then he turned out the light. There was more darkness.

It was midnight when our session ended. I was left feeling nothing, as the encounter only slightly exceeded mediocrity. After a while, Mike maneuvered his body to allow me to lie on his chest, an act that most men wouldn't put up with after random sex, and one that I had never been accustomed to. He caressed my shoulders and it became a moment meant for couples, two people who actually gave a damn about each other – not us. It was quiet again. I guess he expected for me to ask the most dreaded question any female can ask a man, what are you thinking about? I didn't. I lay there, taking in everything, catching my breath and following the trail of sweat that beaded on my forehead and had made its way down my cheek and to the back of my neck. He checked the time on his cell phone, which made me conscious of how late it was getting. I kissed him on his neck, a kind gesture, and jumped out of bed.

"Where you goin'?"

"You're taking me to my car." I turned the lights on.

"Now? You can't go in the morning?"

"It is morning. I left my car in the mall parking lot. It's not secure there. And besides, I'm not comfortable being here."

"She's not coming home."

"Who said I was worried?" I sat on the edge of the bed in my panties and pinned my hair tightly into a bun.

13

Trickery

"So, you like tattoos, huh?" he asked, referring to the letters M-A-K tattooed behind my right ear.

"No actually, I don't." I bent down to put on my shoes.

"He must have been special then."

"You can say that," I removed the pins from my bun and my hair, which fell matted and tangled below my shoulders, hiding the tattoo.

During the ride to my car, Mike found something more to talk about besides the shows. We talked about college sports and politics, primarily. He never mentioned his wife, which sparked my curiosity. I wouldn't be the one to ask. He had done enough for one night, and so had I. At this hour, I was only good for showering and diving head-first onto the couch once I got home.

The fully loaded white Lexus with dark, tinted windows was the only car left in the parking lot, untouched. I sighed with relief, and then reached into my Louis Vuitton handbag to fish out my keys.

"That's your ride?" He pointed at the car.

"Yeah, for now."

"That's nice." I went to pull the latch of the door when he

tugged at my dress.

"Aren't you forgetting something?"

"What?" He pulled a fold of money from a compartment beneath his navigation system and attempted to hand it to me. "What's that?"

"Gas money," he grinned.

"Gas is expensive, but I know it doesn't cost that much. I only live 10 minutes away."

"You know what I mean. Just take the money."

"You think I'm trickin'? Do I look like a prostitute to you?" His eyes widened. "As stupid as it was, I was with you tonight because I wanted to be." I opened the door and let myself out.

He sat there and watched as I walked to my car in the dark, desolate lot. I thought for a moment about the other women with whom he had made similar exchanges and I second-guessed myself. I should've taken the money, but I felt that I wouldn't miss it. It was nothing that I couldn't make up by doing a single show, so I held tightly to that morsel of dignity.

Trickery

Chapter Three

Trickery

The steam from the shower relaxed every muscle in my body, including the one between my thighs. Mike didn't call to make sure I made it home safely, which I didn't mind, so I turned my phone off to get a good night's rest. It was already Monday morning and I only planned three shows for the end of the week. I spent most of my free time in the mall when it wasn't too crowded, so I planned to spend time shopping around for costumes when I awoke. I hadn't been lying down for three minutes when I felt myself dozing off.

That night I dreamed I lived in a mansion, and my husband – yes, husband – was extremely successful. I can't recall his profession, but he was handsome and had a gorgeous smile. The scene was very dark, yet I felt content. I went to the kitchen to microwave popcorn and discovered a baby sitting in a fetal position on the turntable inside. My screams inside the dream jolted my body from the sofa in reality. I couldn't force myself back to sleep afterward, so I watched a few early morning sitcoms until there was sunlight outside my window.

By noon, the sun was completely hidden by dark clouds and the wind had blown numerous tree limbs into the streets. Although

I dressed and prepped for a day at the mall, I decided not to go. My phone flashed red to indicate that I had unchecked voicemail messages. It was Shai, a close associate who I hung out with on occasion, especially if she was paying. The place to be that evening was at her house on the west side of town, and since I had no prior arrangements, it was no question whether or not I would be there. We called them sets. It wasn't large enough to be considered a party, or intimate enough to be considered a social gathering amongst friends. Each set drew a different crowd of eight to 12 people who didn't know each other prior to the engagement.

I spent the majority of the day trying to beautify myself without professional help. I washed my hair and twisted it so that I would have long, wavy strands once untwisted. I shaved my legs, gave myself a manicure and pedicure, exercised a bit – fifty squats, sixty crunches, twenty pushups – just enough to keep my body tight. I threw on a tight pair of jeans, a halter, a pair of flip flops and left for Shai's house.

Shai's place was like walking into a whore house. There were four bedrooms, all void of adequate furnishings. Only hers held a bed and dresser. Visitors placed sheets and blankets along the floors in the event they decided to stay the night, have an orgy or a quickie with a complete stranger. Shai was the only child of a doctor-teacher couple. Not even private school could change her. It only made her want the quick, hood life more than the average street kid. And her parents' white-collar occupations afforded her more expensive drugs than the typical marijuana plant.

16

Trickery

I waited outside for someone to let me into the house after pounding my fist against the door twice. Shai was generally the last person I saw when I entered her house, as was the case that day.

"What's up?" A tall guy opened the door, sporting a faded Chicago Bulls jersey and some outdated Jordan's. His eyes barely open, he pressed his body weight against the door and almost fell to the floor.

"I'm Taj," I said, annoyed.

"And?" He couldn't even look at me.

"Nigga, let me in! I'm Shai's friend." I stormed past him and clutched my Dooney & Bourke bag closer to my side. He closed the door and disappeared to another room.

The space was cloudy. You could barely make out the furniture from all the smoke. The 52-inch television screen flashed artificial light throughout the living room. I couldn't make out the picture on the screen. There were three unfamiliar bodies on the couch as I walked into the living room; all three heads hung loosely from the bodies that held them, staring off into the cloud. Getting closer, I noticed that one of them was a girl.

"Shai?" I asked hesitantly, fearing I would be wrong.

"Naw, shorty. She in the last room on the left."

Music was blaring from the back of the house, and became louder as I approached the final bedroom. I knocked. No one answered. The music was deafening.

"Shai?" I opened the door slowly.

"Come in," someone moaned. I had yet to see a face.

I opened the door wider, and there was a girl. Very tan, she wore a long, loose-fitted, spaghetti strap dress with her hair curled and pinned up loosely into a bun, revealing a butterfly tattooed on her left shoulder. Her legs were crossed, sexy and seductive. She was focused on something else in the room that had not been revealed to me, paying me no attention. I wondered for a moment if she invited me in.

She sat in a corner of the room near a dresser, a mirror, a nightstand and an artificial plant. Then I noticed the head and footboard of a bed followed by Shai in plain view. She was engaging in sexual activity with someone I did not know, and the girl in the chair was merely an audience. She still didn't move. I walked past her, partially in hopes that I could snatch her interests from the show, but also to get a look at the plethora of dope that was laid across the nightstand. There were pills for the pill poppers: white, blue, and green. There was coke, for those who were into that kind of thing. And weed for those who played it safe. I went for the little blue pill and crushed it between my wisdom teeth, a quicker effect, and swallowed with as much saliva as I could create. Then I grabbed a bottle of water, still in the cellophane wrapping beside the bed.

I moved closer to the dresser, turned, reached behind myself and lifted my body to sit on it. My feet dangled two feet from the floor. Not before long, I felt tingling in my temples, an indication that the ecstasy was beginning to take effect. I pressed the back of my head against the mirror hinged to the dresser, then slowly adjusted myself for a better view. My focus wasn't on Shai and her taking a good pounding from the back. I had seen that numerous times before. I stared at the girl in the chair, and if she took offense,

I planned to blame my behavior on the drugs I ingested. The music stopped and Shai's wails filled the air. It sounded painful.

It was hard to rip my eyes from the woman in the chair. She only lost my attention when my high escalated and I could barely raise my eyes. For a while, she was like a portrait, still and unresponsive. Her lips turned up at the corners, and then she reached for the water bottle near her ankle on the floor. She glanced my way, then stood up from her chair and walked toward me.

"What you lookin' at?" she whispered directly into my ear. I noticed Shai had stopped on the bed and was nearly passed out.

"You," I flirted. She leaned in and placed her left hand next to my thigh, slightly touching it.

"Like what you see? Or can you see? How many?" She held up three fingers. Her gold tennis bracelet slid down her tiny wrist.

"One," I replied, eyes half closed.

"Oh my. You'll have to do better than that."

"There is only one of you. I can't focus my attention elsewhere." She lowered her head so I could barely see her smiling. "Don't blush. That's nothing new to you."

"And what makes you say that?" she asked, still grinning.

"If you don't know, then I don't either. What's your name?" I began to stroke her arm uncontrollably. The effects of the drugs were overpowering. She did not move. She leaned in closer, lifted her hand and interlocked it with mine. We slowly caressed each other's hands with our fingertips.

"It's Santina. Everyone calls me San."

"Maybe I'll call you Tina."

"Maybe. You wanna go somewhere and talk?"

"This is somewhere, but if you mean privately, sure, yeah, I'll go."

She grabbed my hand as if to help me down from the dresser. My body became heavier as I landed on my feet. I stroked my hair compulsively, seeming to feel each individual strand flowing through my fingers. I held on to San's arm for balance and we walked out of the room.

We sat on the carpeted hallway floor, on opposite walls, beneath the clouds of smoke. It was quiet. There was no one else there.

"You never told me your name."

"Did you ever ask for it?" We spoke as if in battle.

"Why are you so difficult? What's your name?"

18

Trickery

"I'm teasing. My name is Taj."

"And how you spell that?"

"T-A-J."

"Sounds like a boy's name. Not a name for someone as pretty as you."

"Uh huh. She flirts!" I laughed faintly, barely having enough focus or strength to keep my posture against the wall.

"So, who do you know here?" she asked.

"Shai is my homegirl. We went to school together."

"Really? I didn't take you for the private school type."

"It wasn't private. Where do you think she got her ruggedness from? Not some nun singing hymnals."

San laughed. "I doubt that would be the case, but ok," and she continued to giggle.

"Do you know the guy that's in there?"

"A little. Met him last time I was here," she hung her head, "Shai and her damn boy toys."

"Jealous?"

"Nah, not at all. I don't have a problem getting who I want," she looked directly at me, "if I want them bad enough."

"And a bit arrogant too. Hmm. I kinda' like that."

"Don't be too flattered," she straightened her dress then crossed one leg over the other. I was silent. "I have someone at home."

"A girl?" I asked.

"I'm talking to you, aren't I?" she smiled. "Her name is Kendra. What about you?"

"No one," I said faintly. With the help of the wall, I lifted myself from the floor and threw my bag over my shoulder.

"Shhh…wait…what's that sound?" she looked puzzled.

"What sound?" I looked around.

"It sounds like water. Is it raining?"

"No, it's the lake, you know, behind the house."

"There is a lake back there? I've never seen it."

"Well, it's not too well lit. You can barely see it at night, but if you're quiet enough you can hear it." I pulled my keys from my purse.

"Where you going? You leaving?"

"Yeah, I've been here for two hours now and I gotta work," I lied.

"Time does fly when you're getting high." She smirked.

19

Trickery

"Well – well, I was thinking that maybe we could jump in the lake or something." I shook my head in disagreement, hoping that she was only playfully asking me to jump into a large body of water with freshly sewn in Indian Remy hair. I think she was serious. "But can you drive yourself? You're really messed up."

"I wouldn't recommend that lake to anyone. Who knows what's in there. And I'm a big girl. I can drive. Tell Shai I said to call Taj."

"I know your name. You don't have to remind me," she said with an attitude.

I didn't say goodbye to her. I didn't care to look back as I walked closer to the front door. For all I knew her head was still pressed against the wall as her high escalated in the darkness behind her eyelids. I felt hurt and rejected, even without purpose. Rejection on any level forced me to examine myself, my worthiness to have what others had. It wasn't that San was involved with someone; it was simply that I was not. And that was something that performing shows couldn't help me purchase. Almost as much as I resented relationships, I hated the idea of lacking something even more.

With each step toward the door, I felt my chest become heavy, resting in the pit of my stomach until the weight and disappointment forced tears down my cheek. I didn't stop for a moment to question my behavior until I was outside approaching my car. Then I realized and thought to myself, I'm high as hell.

Trickery

Chapter Four

It was Wednesday, two weeks later, when I received a phone call from Shai. I was sitting in the chair at Happy Nails, a Korean nail salon, having eyelash extensions applied when I felt the phone vibrating beneath my thigh.

"Hello?" I answered, eyes closed tightly.

"Girl, whatchu doin'?"

"Getting my eyelashes put on."

"Oh, you want me to let you go?"

"No, girl, you ok. Damn, it's been a minute. It took you this long to call me?"

"Girl, I've been busy. Anyway, let me tell you. Someone been blowin' me up to get your number," she paused, thinking I would ask who it was. "You wanna know who?"

"If you wanna tell me."

"My friend, San."

"You mean, Tina?"

"I don't think she goes by that – anyway, I told her I wouldn't give her your number, so I'm finally calling you to give you hers." She paused. "You want it?"

"Text it to me. I can't see right now, remember?"

"Alright then. I gotta go. Bye." She hung up.

I didn't expect for Shai to text the number to me immediately, and if she had I probably would have waited another week anyway to call San. As far as I knew, we had little to nothing in common and to top it off, she was in a relationship. It took Shai three days to text the phone number to me. I assume San called to find out if Shai had delivered the message, then Shai finally followed through. And I still waited a week.

It was almost 3:00 a.m. when I placed the first phone call to San. I'd had a long night working with Tiki and I needed to hear a voice other than rappers on the stereo. I settled into my car, double-checked that I had all my earnings for that night, and then stuffed it into the glove box. I fastened my seatbelt and then dialed her number.

"Hello?" she said, wide awake.

"Why aren't you asleep?"

"I just got in. I went out tonight."

"Where'd you go? Wait, first, do you know who this is?"

"Of course I do. I went to a night club near the beach."

"Sounds fun." There was silence. "Well, I don't want to keep you up, just talk to you briefly and—"

"What are you doing tomorrow?" she cut me off.

"Nothing. Why?"

"Make sure you call me. I want to see you."

"Ok. Make sure you answer."

We said our goodbyes and both ended the call.

After waking up around noon the following day, I noticed I had three text messages from San. I called her without reading a single one and made arrangements to meet up at my favorite bookstore near the mall. I didn't want to overdo it, so with a bare face and a pair of large-framed sunglasses, I threw on a tight pair of Lucky Brand jeans, a J'adore Dior top and sprayed a bit of perfume.

We pulled up to the bookstore at the same time. She noticed me first and signaled by honking the horn of her new midnight blue Toyota Camry, which was a bit goofy, but I figured she was anxious. We exited our cars quickly and made our way to the door. She wore a tight pair of light blue jeans with rips and tears throughout, along with a waist-length black halter. She had applied her make-up lightly for daytime wear, which only minimally enhanced her natural beauty.

We greeted each other with a hug and went straight to the row of books that we found most appealing.

"Why is it that African American fiction books have pictures of half-naked women on them?" she asked as she picked up a book from the shelf.

"I think it has something to do with what appeals to the urban community. Think about it," she looked at me, "what's in most hip-hop videos?"

"Oh, I see. Well, we'll never see a Danielle Steele book with a half-naked white woman on it." We both giggled.

"You ever wonder why bookstores designate a section for African American fiction? Or what makes a book African American fiction, the writer being black or the book's content?" She looked baffled.

"So, you read a lot?" she asked.

"Yeah, in my spare time," I said, browsing the Omar Tyree section.

"What do you read?"

"Anything that can keep my interest long enough to get through it, but I really like books that can teach me something though."

"I've been writing for a while now – nothing major, but I've never been big on reading. I'll put a book down after a few chapters and never pick it up again," she volunteered.

"Perhaps you weren't reading the right books, good books."

She walked to the opposite side of the shelf and fingered through a couple of novels. From time to time, we would both glance up from the never-ending rows of books and catch each other's eyes. I couldn't see her lips, but her eyes smiled back at mine. I picked up the latest E. Lynn Harris novel and walked around the corner to join her.

"Ready?"

"If you are," she answered. "Is that what you came here for?"

"Maybe. I won't know what I like until I've read it."

She shrugged her shoulders and led the way to the cash register. We made plans to go to the mall after leaving the bookstore. She wanted to look for a gift for her mother's birthday, and I didn't mind picking up a few things. She got into the BMW I had rented for that week and left her car in the bookstore parking lot.

23

Trickery

She was quiet for most of the ride, only turning down the music once to compliment me on having such a nice car. I smiled and said "thank you", but it was too soon for her to know about what I had and how I had come to have it. She looked from the passenger side window as if she were hoping that someone would save her. From the way she would focus most of her attention on drivers of other cars, crossing pedestrians, and buildings we'd passed, I felt like I was kidnapping her and she wanted to finger "HELP" in a heavily fogged window.

"Are you ok?" I turned down some old school Keith Sweat I had been playing all week.

"Yeah. Why you ask?" She continued to look from the window.

"Well – because of that." I raised my hand to indicate her demeanor. "It's like you're looking for someone to save you. If you're uncomfortable or something, I can take you back to your car."

"No, I'm fine. I guess there are a few things on my mind."

And I didn't bother to ask about those things. I figured if she wanted me to know she would offer that information. We rode the rest of the way in silence, but once we arrived at the mall, she wouldn't stop talking. Every outfit put her in mind of one of her friends – the whore, the conservative, the church girl, and even herself. From time to time I would drift away from her just to hear her voice dying down in the distance. I could tell she may have been a little nervous and had to constantly find something to say to avoid the common awkwardness of hanging out with someone for the first time. And it wasn't upsetting, just irritating.

"Ahh, that's cute." She came from behind.

"Yeah, isn't it?" I held up a pair of khaki shorts made for toddler.

"So you got a kid, huh?" she picked up a different pair of shorts from the rack. "I have a daughter, too. Her name is —"

"I never said I had a kid." I turned and walked away.

"Well, my daughter's name is Sarai," she followed behind me.

"Isn't that a biblical name?" I asked.

"Yeah. She was Abraham's wife in the book of Genesis, who was so beautiful that Abraham had to tell the Egyptians that she was his sister in order to avoid being killed. And —."

"I know the story." I cut her off. "And where is your daughter?"

24

Trickery

I asked, stopping to look at clothes on a different rack.

"My mom's. I just need to get myself together then I'm going to get her. I can't wait to bring her home to me. You have no idea."

Oh, but I do, I thought.

She went on to tell me how her ex-boyfriend would abuse her and Sarai, and that once she was able to support and protect her daughter, she would take her from her parents' home. Sarai became the topic of the afternoon. By the end of our time at the mall, I had learned her favorite color, things to eat, cartoons, books and games. It was obvious that San had a sort of emptiness and remorse for her situation with her daughter. I felt sorry for her; the beautiful creature she was, with so much hindering her from reaching her fullest potential. She had worked in the public library for a year and barely made enough money to pay her bills. Before that day, I wondered what solace drugs and alcohol offered her, what void needed to be filled there, and then I discovered it. Her confiding in me was beyond anything that I could fathom. She talked to me as though we were old friends. I learned more about her in a few hours than I had learned about close acquaintances I knew for years.

San was the youngest of three, and the only daughter. She was raised like any other black, middle-class child. Both of her parents were still together, and as far as she knew, still happy with each other. She wrote poetry like nothing I'd ever heard before and truly embraced her artistic side. I realized that San was nothing like me, which I envied at times. She possessed an innocence that contrasted greatly to everything I was, and it was undeniably appealing.

She was honest, and never held back the details no matter how disturbing the truth may have been. I, on the other hand, kept myself in enough darkness to hide what I feared would allow someone access into my world.

We'd made plans to see each other, and we kept each of them: dinner on Tuesday, lunch on Thursday, a movie on Friday. After a month, my time became divided between work and San. I never questioned the relationship she informed me she'd had when we first met, putting it off as pretense. Besides, we didn't consider furthering whatever our relationship was; we both simply filled a void in each other's life. I saw beauty throughout San, and although I greatly acknowledged her physical attributes, it was not that she had eyes as beautiful as Saharan sands, but the way she looked at me with them; not that her calves and thighs were tight and toned, but how her walk defined her confidence; the way she smiled, touched and talked as though we were old friends. I found no faults with her, but even so, I kept my guard up.

26

Trickery

Chapter Five

San invited me to a poetry spot downtown one Saturday
evening. She wanted me to hear a new piece that she'd written, so
I agreed to go along. I packed a duffle bag in preparation for work
that evening and called Tiki to make sure that she would be in
place. She had yet to fall through on our plans, but I had to be sure
that I would be able to make some money. San and I went back
and forth on the phone that evening while she coached me through
getting to the proper location. She was excited. It could be heard
in her voice. When I pulled up, she stood outside, wearing jeans
and a crisp, collared shirt and holding a red notebook.

"Thank you for coming." She reached out to hug me.

"No problem. I wanted to see what this was all about."

"You'll like it. Believe me, everyone does."

"Oh, someone is stripping?" I asked, playfully.

"What? No. Don't be silly. You'll like this."

We walked inside and were seated to the right of the stage.
There were candles placed on each table, emitting the only source
of light for the space. There were several couples, a few groups
of friends who spoke loudly amongst their parties and a few who
were promoting a book or selling their performance pieces on

CD. The host walked from table to table to greet everyone in the audience. I felt that my presence there was greatly appreciated.

After 15 minutes, the emcee took stage and announced the poets for the evening, one by one, as they each went up to perform. Performers read numerous poems about love, or the lack of, some about ridiculous jobs and others about the revolution, which perplexed many audience members. San stared at the pages in her notebook the entire time she waited to be called. She only looked up and snapped at the very end of each performance, as though she were able to read and listen to each performer simultaneously.

"Let's hear it again for D. Truth, ladies and gentlemen," the emcee announced.

"Next, we're going to hear from a little lady who has been performing here with us for the past year. She's going to bless us tonight with a new piece." He looked at her. "San, you're up. Give it up for her, ladies and gentlemen."

She gave me a nervous smile and rose from the table. I gave her a smirk in response and watched as she walked away, touching the backs of people she knew along the way.

"Ya'll a'ight?" She started.

The audience replied with a loud, "Yeah!"

Trickery

For a moment I felt like a character in Alex Hairston's Love Don't Come Easy. She nervously turned the pages in her notebook before she began.

"This piece is not yet titled." She looked from the notebook to the audience. "Even my – thoughts become unclear as I – strain to express myself with word – stuttering unto paper – never thinking imaginable that I would be here – enraptured in this sea of confusion and self-misguidance —"

I had never heard her perform. She was different, completely transformed. Her voice demanded the attention of everyone in the room. Her body language made her seriousness clear and evident. There were a few snaps in the middle of her piece, but I didn't catch what she'd said. As clear as they were, I was lost in her words. She ended the piece with a flirty smile and a "thank you," and then made her way back to the table, smiling as though she had a sense of relief.

"You were great, San. Were you nervous?"

"Well, of course. I always get butterflies before I go up. Then I'm okay once I get started." She grabbed my hand. "But did you really like it?"

"Yeah, it was one of the best ones tonight."

"Well, it was about us."

"Us?" I was appalled. I hadn't heard the entire poem.

"Yeah." She nodded and smiled.

The emcee spoke again and for a moment I was saved.

"Let's listen to the next one. We'll talk about yours later on, okay?"

She nodded her head again.

Two performers had gone up and San and I didn't say anything to each other. I checked my phone and realized that time had passed quickly. I was supposed to meet Tiki at 11:30 p.m. for work that night, so I had to say goodbye to San.

I gently tugged at her shirt to get her attention. She turned to me, eyes wide.

"I have to go," I mouthed and pointed to the door.

"Now?" she asked.

She reached for my hand but I pulled back, "I have to work."

She looked disappointed and motioned to walk out of the room where we could hear each other and not distract others. Once outside, she stood in front of me and folded her arms. "Where are you going, Taj?"

Trickery

"I'm curious to know what puts you in a position to question me." Her jaw dropped a little. "But if you must know, I'm going to work. I have to work tonight."

"You don't have to be so damn cold towards me, Taj." She turned as if she would walk away, and then stopped in her tracks. "Ah man, come on. What is this, Taj? What's going on?" It appeared that she would cry.

"What? What do you mean?" I pretended to not understand her sudden outburst of emotion.

"I try my hardest to not question anything that you do. You're so secretive, you know. I don't know where you live or where you work. I've spent almost every day with you. Why — why am I an outsider?"

Her emotions transferred to me. I realized how much I had kept her out of any and everything that had to do with me. I didn't feel that I was obligated to let her in, but I felt remorse knowing that she did not deserve the treatment I dished out to her. No one was ever so eager to know those things about me, and only accepted what I offered them.

"I'm not ready to tell you yet, San. Understand that." I said, placing my hand on her right shoulder.

"Are you a prostitute or something?" I looked away from her. "Are you?"

"No, I'm not!" I was a bit angered by her question.

"And?" she asked, waiting for me to respond, but I offered nothing. "We can't be friends," she said, shaking her head.

At that moment, I thought about waking up the following day and not hearing her voice, or sharing another meal with her, or even exchanging one good book with her for another one. More importantly, I thought about the void, the inescapable emptiness that existed before I met her. I couldn't endure having such a gaping hole in my life again. I wasn't afraid of losing her, but I was afraid of experiencing loss.

"Let's go," I grabbed her hand and rushed toward the door, fearing I would be late.

She didn't say anything on the ride to the hotel. She sat there with her arms folded, staring out the window. Ten minutes later, we arrived at the Hyatt downtown on the river. She evaluated her surroundings, and by the look on her face, I figured she believed her assumptions were right and that I was indeed a prostitute. I parked in the garage adjacent to the hotel and told San to get out. I went to the trunk and pulled out my duffle bag.

30

Trickery

"No, I'm not an assassin if that's what you're thinking," I said, trying to lighten the mood. She didn't say anything.

We took the elevator to the sixth floor and walked down the corridor to room 623. San followed me in. Tiki sprung from the bathroom in powder blue lingerie and black patent leather pumps, putting on an earring.

"Girl, where you been? You were supposed to be here a half hour ago. Hurry up and get dressed." She walked back into the bathroom without noticing that someone else was in the room.

"Sit over there," I said firmly and pointed to a chair in the corner, "and please don't wander around. Don't talk to anyone."

"But there is no one else here," she said, confused.

"Listen to me." I walked up to her, our noses only inches apart. "Please – please don't judge me." She broke eye contact with me and sat down. What shocked me most was my own behavior – I actually cared what she thought of me. Was I deeply ashamed of myself?

I showered and dressed quickly, nervous that San would be exposed to some drunken crowd that assumes every woman in the room is a part of the show. Before I exited the bathroom, Tiki had already begun to play music. I assumed that the night's crowd was already arriving. "Oh God – San." I was about to open my world up to her and it made me sick to my stomach. There was no need for a drink; I couldn't have felt higher, or more nausea for that matter.

A crowd had gathered around the bed where Tiki was sitting. All attention was on her half-naked body. The bathroom door creaked as I closed it behind myself, and a few turned to look. San sat up in her chair, examining my body; the black fishnet stockings connected to the hot pink garter belt with matching bra and thong. My body glistened in pure jojoba oil. My hair was pinned so that only a few strands fell in my face. All eyes were then on me.

San watched my every movement in fascination. She had never seen me without my clothes, and, I assume, was extremely curious about what I was about to do without them. Her eyes jumped from Tiki, back to me, then to Tiki again. It became evident that she had figured it out. She sat back in her chair.

Tiki laid down the rules: no touching, jacking off, rudeness, ignorance or loudness. The price was $150 that night, because of the niceness of the hotel. The men dug into their pockets and threw the money on the bed. Tiki collected it, and it was time to begin.

Trickery

We both kneeled on the bed, facing each other. Her lace, one-piece costume covered only her nipples. I was excited, so I went for them, grabbing and sucking, flicking her nipples with the tip of my tongue. She moaned. I slid a hand between her thighs and stroked her, applying a bit of pressure where I assumed her clit would be. She pressed harder against my hand. It excited me more. I grabbed her waist and kissed her, then flung her body down on the bed, showing some aggression. I gently put my hand on her right knee and slowly pulled her right leg toward me, opening her legs enough to give the crowd a look. We continued kissing as I slid my finger inside her. She gripped my forearm tightly and pushed it in deeper.

I had gotten so lost in what was going on in the show that I forgot about my guest that night. Tiki and I were maneuvering each other on the bed, a sexy transition, and I looked out into the crowd for San. The chair in the back of the room was empty. I scanned our audience; she was nowhere in sight. She was gone. I couldn't seem distracted at that point. It was a situation I would have to deal with at a later time.

After the show, Tiki and I packed up and said our goodbyes to the guys. I had every intention of calling San as soon as it was all over, but I realized that I'd left my cell phone in the car. I just wanted to make sure that she was okay and that we were still cool with each other.

It was almost 2:00 a.m., and the hotel lobby was empty. No one was coming or going; even the reception desk was deserted. The door slid open automatically and I walked out. San was sitting on the curb; shoulders slouched forward, arms resting on her thighs.

"Hey you." I stood next to her.

"What's up?" She pulled at her fingertips.

"Wow! Is it that bad?" I laughed faintly.

"You know, the only reason I'm still here is because my purse is in your car and I couldn't get a taxi to get away from here without it. So, please," she stood up and dusted the back of her jeans, "if you would give me my purse I could —"

"Wait a minute. You wanted to see this. I didn't bring you here to upset you."

"Just give me my purse."

"No, you're not going anywhere like this." My concern surprised me as much as it surprised her. "And you can be damn sure I'm not letting you take a taxi this late."

"Oh, like you give a damn about someone else besides yourself now?"

"What? Where is this coming from?"

"Just get my damn purse."

"I'm lost." I pressed my hand against my forehead, confused. "I'm not giving you anything! I thought we were cool, San. I thought you would understand." I paused for a moment. "You know, this is my fault." I reached inside my handbag and withdrew my car keys. "I knew it. This is why I don't let people in."

"Is that what you think you did, Taj? Let me in?"

"Come on. Get your purse." I started to walk away.

"Is that it?" She placed her hands on her hips.

"It's what you wanted, isn't it?" I stopped and turned to her.

"No, no it's —"

"What then?" I yelled.

"It's you. It's you that I want, Taj. Can you not see past all the walls you have built up around yourself? I've never met anyone so beautiful, but so damn stupid to realize when someone genuinely

32

Trickery

cares about them." There was silence as I stared out into the street. "You know, just get my purse."

There was no response on my end. I walked to the car, and unlocked the doors by keyless entry.

"It's open," I said.

She reached in through the passenger side, pulled out her purse and threw it over her shoulder. By the time I placed my bag in the trunk she had disappeared. I looked around the lot, into the darkness. There wasn't a single shadow. "San?" I called. There wasn't a response.

There was no movement in the parking lot. I shined the headlights, on high beam, in the vicinity around the hotel. She was gone.

There wasn't a single part of me that believed San was being sincere. We were close acquaintances, and even that was new to me. Of course there was some attraction to her on my end, but I had made up in my mind at some point to keep my distance from her. What could I offer her? I thought.

It had only been 24 hours since I last heard from San, but I already felt that something was missing. The void quickly came back into plain sight. Considering that I had been with her almost every day for weeks, I knew that it would be difficult without her for a while. Then I counted that day as day one towards the recovery process and thought pretty soon she'll just be considered another person of my past.

33

Trickery

Chapter Six

I sat in the farthest, quietest corner of the bookstore reading one of the latest releases in African American fiction. It was late, 9:00 p.m. perhaps. I was so consumed with the book that I lost track of time. To preview a book that I was intending to purchase, to me, meant that I would have to read at least the first three chapters. By then, I had read five. It was indeed a must-have. I walked to the counter, reaching in my purse for some cash to make a purchase.

"How are you this evening?" the cashier asked.

"Good." I replied, still digging through my purse. I found a $20 bill and finally took notice of the person behind the register. She was beyond gorgeous. She had the cutest dimples and her smile was close to perfect. Her skin was a flawless shade of brown and her hair was jet-black and flowing, to her shoulders. I handed her the book.

"Oh, this is a good one. I've read it before."

"Really?" She nodded. "Then that means we have the same taste in books."

"Maybe so."

"I wonder what else we have in common." I smiled, trying to

make her feel comfortable about a woman making passes at her.

"Who knows," she shrugged her shoulders.

"What's your name?" I asked.

"Brandi."

"Oh, I see. It says it right there on your—" my eyes were fixed on her chest.

Then, I heard a voice coming from behind me. "Don't mind her. She's a big flirt." It was a familiar voice that I had not heard in a while. I turned quickly.

"San?" She was behind me holding some children's books, wearing an extremely large smile.

"What? Thought you would never run into me?"

"Yes – no. I mean —." She moved past me, to the register.

"I would like these please," she told the cashier.

"I mean, it's been weeks. How have you been?"

"If you wanted to know the answer to that, you would have called me weeks ago."

"Are you still mad?" I thought about it for a moment. "You didn't call me either." The cashier tried hard to pretend she wasn't listening.

Trickery

"I was never mad at you." She picked up her bag and took her receipt, "Thank you."

"Then what was it?" I followed close behind her.

"If you don't know the answer to that, then —"

"Why are you so hard with me now?" It seemed as if the tables had turned.

"Listen." She turned to look at me. "It's not a big deal to me anymore." She smirked. "We're still cool. As a matter of fact, I was going to have a drink across the street. Do you wanna go?" She paused for a moment. "Oh, or do you have to work?" she said sarcastically.

"No, I don't."

"Come on then."

We walked out together. Our cars were parked next to each other, but she wouldn't have known. That week's rental was a midnight blue Jaguar, one of my favorite rides. We took her car to the bar directly across the street from the bookstore and ordered one drink after another: a top shelf margarita, a blue Long Island, a few shots of Patron and even a Jell-O shot or two. It seemed like forever since I last spoke to San. I didn't realize how much I actually missed her until she was in my presence again. We didn't discuss the events of that night. It was like it never happened, and we picked up exactly where we left off. She talked about how she was closer to getting her daughter to come home with her and how she was working at the poetry spot as a server for some extra cash. There was nothing new going on with me. It was always the same with me.

"I don't think you should be driving now," I said, "let me take you home."

"I'm fine." She could barely keep her eyes open. "You don't have your car anyway."

"I can drive you home."

"No. I'm fine. Thank you though."

"Are you sure? I really don't think —"

"Yeah – actually, you can drive me – to your house." I looked serious. "My house?"

"Exactly. We're friends, right?"

"I mean — yeah. That's no problem."

"Really?" she seemed stunned that I agreed. "Let's go then," she said, possibly fearing that I would change my mind.

She could barely walk in the parking lot. I drove back to the bookstore and changed cars. I figured it would be more of a liability if I left the rental there overnight. I helped her into the passenger seat of the car and she immediately put her head back, hardly noticing that she was in a different car. I had never invited anyone into my apartment, but it would be the price I'd pay for her companionship, anything to prevent her from disappearing again. Or perhaps revealing more of my lifestyle would have an adverse effect and drive her farther from me. It was risky.

She was on the verge of passing out. I put her arm across my shoulder and held her waist to help her into the apartment. I made a place for her on the sofa. My bedroom was always a mess, so I threw some pillows and a freshly washed comforter on the sofa and helped her to it. She didn't move, only gave a drunken moan here and there. The room was quiet, except for the clock on the wall that made a tick tock sound that wouldn't have seemed so loud had my senses not been heightened by the alcohol. I could feel the hairs standing in my ears with each stroke. The sound was like a drum. I lay on a blanket next to her on the floor until I eventually fell asleep.

37

Trickery

"Wake up, sleepy." The sun was up and so was San. She leaned over the edge of the sofa and touched my face with the back of her hand.

"What time is it?"

"Morning."

"Ha ha. Very funny."

"You asked. Are we at your place?"

"Yeah. This is where you wanted to go, right?"

"Um, yeah. It's comfortable." She looked around at the few pieces of furniture sporadically placed around the living room. "I like your couch, but why aren't we in bed?" She was very forward.

"It's a mess back there. And I wouldn't want you to wake up and —"

"Can I see?" She was like an Energizer bunny. She moved the covers from her body.

"Did you have a cup of coffee or something already this morning?" She jumped up from the couch and walked down the hallway to the bedroom and opened the door. "Don't say I didn't warn you," I yelled from the living room.

"Wow! You're right. You sure have a lot of clothes and shoes, but the room is very spacious." Her voice gradually became lower, an indication that she was getting deeper into the room. "What's this?"

I got up from the floor and rushed into the bedroom.

She was holding a blue blanket and standing over a small brown box tucked off in the corner.

"That? That's nothing," I said, trying to take it from her.

"No, wait a minute," she snatched back, "Micah Anthony Kingston," she said, reading what was stitched into the blanket.

"Give it to me." She could tell I was getting upset.

"Come here." I took a step forward. She quickly reached for my hair and lifted it from my neck. "M-A-K," she said aloud.

"I know. Please don't —."

"I won't judge you, if that's what you're thinking. I just know that you have a lot of secrets and day after day I'm discovering them." She dropped the blanket back into the box. "So how old is he?"

"Again with the questions! Who are you? FBI or

something?"

"You're so full of it. I don't feel bad for asking a question that a normal person wouldn't have a hard time answering."

"He's five now," I answered, aggravated.

"Is he with his father? Your parents?" She folded her arms.

"Look, I don't have time to be questioned by you. This whole thing was a bad idea." I turned to walk away and she grabbed my arm.

"No. Stop walking away from me. Just talk to me, Taj. I only want to understand what's going on with you. Why you do the things you do. What makes you — drives you."

"Don't give me poetry. My life is real. You wouldn't understand that."

"And so is mine. What do you want me to do?"

"Just be what I want you to be," I uttered from somewhere.

"What? And what's that?" she laughed faintly.

"Just be there — here. That's it."

"No. You can't dictate how people act, what they say and what they do. We put up with who and what people are, or we don't. It's that simple."

"I was raped, San. My mom died when I was a kid and who the hell knows who my dad is. My foster parents couldn't have given a damn about me. I lived in that house for three years — three years." She stared at me. "I didn't have anywhere else to go, so a crack house became my place of residency for months. I had nothing."

"Who raped you?" she asked hesitantly.

"My foster brother." I forced it out. "He was older than me, bigger than me, stronger than me. My foster parents didn't listen. They said it was my clothes, the way I wore my hair, the way I walked, how I tiptoed from the shower to my bedroom. It wasn't their son. It was me." I started to fold some of the clothes from the bed in hopes that I would distract her and end her questioning.

"But where is he — the baby?"

"The state has 'em." I found it hard to swallow. I stopped folding clothes for a moment. "He was born with dope in his system." She looked shocked. "I tried but I couldn't cope with everything that I was going through and I lost him." She leaned in to hug me. I rested my head on her shoulder and held her tight.

"Shh now. You'll get him back."

For a moment, I felt that he was better off exactly where he was.

Chapter Seven

I had never spent so much time learning to care for someone, which was the least that I could do for all she'd done for me. Four months passed before either of us realized it. I spent numerous days hiding behind bookshelves, chatting with her at work, and nights rushing performances to make it back to her. Our time was spent talking to each other, indulging in popular novels or old flicks. We frequently took trips to Atlanta, staying at Hilton Downtown and blowing money in strip clubs for the fun of it. There was a trip to New York, and even a cruise to the Western Caribbean. Escaping our day-to-day routine became a day-to-day goal for us, but primarily came at my expense.

Prior to meeting San, I was very keen on my spending habits. Money had become an issue. There were no longer moments that I would decline to do a show. I was desperate for money and had not heard from Tiki in almost a week. Her phone had been disconnected, but I finally received a call one evening as San and I were on the way to dinner at one of our favorite seafood spots near the beach.

"Hello?" No one spoke. "Who is this?"

"Girl, it's me."

"Tiki? Where you been?"

"I'm in Alabama right now. My grandma died and I'm here with my people."

"I'm sorry to hear that," I said, not feeling the least bit remorseful, "so why are you calling?"

"I just wanted to let you know so you won't —"

"Naw, it's cool. Just call when you get back." I hung up. I knew I should have been more understanding, sympathetic even, but she was my only way to make money and she was hours away, which created a huge problem. Part of me even wondered if her grandmother had died at all. Knowing Tiki, she was in the Caribbean with some overweight, buck-toothed, retired athlete who offered her money. That's just how the game was played.

After my conversation with Tiki, I closed the phone then threw it on the dashboard. San grabbed it and asked what was wrong. I offered nothing. At dinner I was extremely quiet, plotting my next move. Robbing a bank was always at the top of my list, but how I would actually pull it off? Then I considered some check-writing scheme that would tie me over until Tiki returned. That idea quickly went out the window when I considered possibly having to pay the money back when or if I was ever caught. One thought led to another and San wasn't the type to talk without someone else contributing to the conversation, so there were moments that neither of us spoke.

Trickery

"So, you're gonna hide something from me?" she asked, stirring her Patrón margarita with a straw.

"I'm not hiding anything. I just don't feel the need to talk about it."

"Why? Maybe I can offer some advice or something."

"Tiki is out of town." I lowered my eyes, knowing I was on the verge of vulnerability. "I need money, but I can't make any without her."

"Do you not know anyone else? Shai, maybe?"

"Hell no! Who would want to see her tacky ass doing a show? We'll have to pay them to watch it," we both chuckled.

"Well," she hesitated, "maybe I can help you."

"I don't want your money San. I can't —"

"No, I can help you with the show," she stared at me. I didn't expect for her to make such an offer.

"But we're friends. I can't mix the two. It's too much. I want to keep things the way they are."

"Well, don't say I didn't offer." She took a sip of her margarita then looked off.

I didn't need a new business partner, or sex partner for that matter, but I was in need of money. I trusted her, and after 15 minutes, I accepted her offer. In that moment, I had no idea how the situation would play out. I should have been happy to have an opportunity to make money, but for the first time I was nervous. I had seen San naked on a few occasions, but not during intimate settings — fitting rooms in clothing stores primarily. I didn't find her body to be sexy, but beautiful. I had searched almost every inch of her body for the slightest flaw. I uncovered none. I imagined kissing the purple butterfly on her left shoulder, and found myself staring at it quite frequently, but a part of me was afraid to touch her.

The rest of the evening was spent contacting some guys that I knew in order to arrange a performance meeting. I managed to scrounge 10 who were willing to pay at least one hundred dollars, making our earnings for that evening – a one hour show – a thousand dollars. San asked numerous questions about the show: Can they touch us? What if they touched us? What if the police officers come? What if we're robbed? What will we wear? I answered all of her questions positively, even if I had never stopped to think of it myself. I wanted her to feel safe, comfortable. Moreover, I wanted to protect her.

Saturday arrived quickly. San and I spent most of the day shopping and getting manicures and pedicures. I had my lashes refreshed by the Koreans while San waited. She despised anything artificial. Her hair and nails were always natural. She wore very little make-up if she ever wore any at all. On the other hand, I openly accepted any enhancements that would make me stand out from the ordinary woman. Not that I couldn't stand out enough without them, but I liked to come across as, or at least feel, untouchable.

We carried our things to the hotel room, a room on the fourth floor of the Hyatt in downtown Jacksonville. San barely said anything. Every once in a while she would release a heavy sigh, and then sip more of the rum and coke she'd mixed in a paper cup. I decided not to drink that night, or be under the influence of anything for that matter, wanting to be aware of everything that was going on around me.

"Should I get dressed now, Taj?" San asked, sitting at the edge

Trickery

of the bed.

"Well, what time is it?"

She looked at her watch. "Almost eight."

"Yeah, you can jump in the shower. Then I'll get in after you."

She stood from the bed and walked over to the overnight bag in the corner of the room and removed some of her belongings. "Where are the razors? I really need to shave."

"Look in the bag by the door. I think I packed them there."

She went into the bathroom and emerged after half an hour, wearing only a towel. Her hair had been pinned into a loose ponytail and her make-up had been applied lightly. Her features resembled those of a doll, exaggerated yet beautiful. I couldn't determine whether or not I wanted to fantasize about her or feel jealous. I was truly torn. I walked past her without speaking and went into the bathroom to prepare myself.

After 20 minutes I was applying make-up behind the locked bathroom door. San attempted to turn the knob.

"Yeah?" I called out.

"Are you almost finished? It's almost nine and —" her voice trembled.

"Don't worry. I'm almost done."

"Well, okay. I'm not opening the door if someone knocks. Just know that."

"That's fine. I'll get it."

She was sitting in the chair next to the bed when I walked from the bathroom. I went over to the corner near her to stuff clothes into the overnight bag. She smelled sweet. Her legs were crossed and I could see every inch of her right thigh. They were extremely toned. Her costume was a simple two-piece, bra and panty set that we picked up at Frederick's of Hollywood in the mall. The set was peach and was lined in brown lace. Her shoes were gold in color which matched her accessories: a gold bangle, hoop earrings and gold necklace dangling two interlocking 'C's.

"You look very nice."

"So do you," she replied.

"Are you ready?"

"Umm hmm," she nodded.

Our first set of guests arrived five minutes after 9. I had never seen this crew at a show before, but it was obvious that the four of them had been at a bar before coming to the hotel. Each of them reeked of alcohol and slurred a little when they spoke, but for the most part, seemed pleasant, like they weren't going to give us a hard time. Two of them walked over to San while she sat in the chair. She leaned forward to shake their hands, loosely gripping. I felt it would be the beginning of a very long night.

Others began to pour in not long afterwards. There were a few familiar faces in the crowd whom I had to introduce to San. By 9:30 p.m. there were 14 guests in the room, and I locked the door in order to begin the show. Since San had never done a show before, I talked the entire time. I laid out all the rules for the night: no touching, grabbing, fighting, jacking off or opening the door during the show. San assisted in collecting our base pay of $1400. Tips would follow.

I signaled for her to go over to the bed, and then I turned off the lights in the back of the room in hopes that it would make her more comfortable if she wasn't able to see some of the guys. I typically kept every light on during a show in order to look out for those breaking the rules, but I figured that I was more alert that night given my sobriety, and that I would catch any awkward activity.

The men were extremely quiet, staring at San on the bed. I pressed play on the stereo and kneeled on the floor between her legs, resting my head on her lap. She caressed my face for a moment, then leaned in and ran her fingers down my back, stopping at my bra strap. I looked up at her and she grabbed my face and slowly moved toward me for a kiss. I braced myself. Our lips pressed softly at first. Her lips were so smooth and plump. I couldn't break away, but pressed harder, longer. I cupped her chin with my right hand, keeping her mouth engaged with mine. Our tongues danced subtly in the space between our lips' meeting place. I lifted myself from the floor – lips still entangled with hers – and helped maneuver her body farther up on the bed.

She crossed her legs while lying flat on her back. My hand began at her tight abdomen and inched down past her panties to her thigh. I whispered, "Let me in." She slowly opened her legs. I made circles on her chest, abdomen, and thighs with my tongue then hesitantly tugged at her panties. Finally, she'd blocked the idea that 14 other people were in the room watching us. She helped me take off her panties, using the tip of her index finger to pull them down her thighs then maneuvering each leg to remove them completely. She moved so seductively, never losing eye

45

Trickery

contact. She moaned subtly, sexy, but any more would have been too much.

She positioned one hand on each of her breasts, massaging them. I reached for her right hand and placed it between her thighs. She began to massage there as well. The men began to stir a little, wanting a closer look. I brought my knees up to a doggy-style position and started to stroke myself. San had flipped a switch within me. I was only inches away, but I refused to sink my head between her thighs. I wanted to start over at her mouth again, kiss her slowly, softly. I did. She wrapped her arms around me, tight. After a few minutes, I made my way down again. I didn't come up for a while.

We switched positions numerous times. We incorporated a toy or two, but we spent most of the time interlocked in a kiss, and before we knew it, an hour and a half had passed. The show was only intended to be an hour long. I finally pried my hands away from her body and reached for my cell phone. "It's over," I whispered to her. She looked disappointed.

By the end of the show we had made almost $300 in tips, bringing our total for that evening to $1700. When the room was clear, San sat up in bed. She was obviously comfortable around me in the nude. She removed the covers and sat straight up, revealing her breasts. A part of me did not want to look at her. I wanted the images of her and I being intimate to be completely erased from my mind and return to just being comfortable enough to talk about anything. What could I have said to her at the point without coming across as awkward?

"So, that was it, huh?" she asked, maneuvering the cover to look at the mess we made.

"Yeah, wasn't much to it." I was putting on a T-shirt, no bra.

"I actually liked it. I got paid to have great sex."

"Easy, right? Here, here is your money." I attempted to hand over $800 in cash.

"What's that for? I said I was helping out. I'm not Tiki."

"Are you sure?" I wasn't going to argue about it.

"Yeah. Why don't you treat me to dinner or something. We'll call it even."

"That won't be a problem."

A week later, I treated her to dinner. We dined over Bang Bang shrimp, fresh salmon and several glasses of wine at Bonefish Grill near the beach, but my encounter with San on the night of the show

Trickery

forced me back a few steps. At one point, we were inseparable, but I found myself ignoring several of her phone calls throughout the day. I thought of her more but wanted to speak with her less.

In some ways, my actions were unexplainable, but what was clear was the presence of emotions that I had not experienced for anyone else in my entire life. I didn't know how to handle them. Of course it was frustrating to her. Several voicemails contained deep sighs of aggravation, which never received a response. I no longer wanted her in a position as my friend. I had to determine how she would fit into my life, if at all. San challenged everything I believed in: that people are naturally selfish beings who would stop at nothing to get ahead and are willing to hurt or leave others behind in the process. She had become too close for comfort, and I rejected it with all my might.

I had spoken to San only twice in a two-week period. When I hadn't heard from her in three days, I became worried. At first I figured that she was over my little game of not answering whenever she called, but when my calls went unanswered, I knew that something was wrong. I called her three times; each one was quickly directed to voicemail. By 8:00 p.m., she had not returned any of my calls or messages. I decided to drive over to her place.

San lived only 20 minutes from my house, but the neighborhoods were extremely different. She lived alone on the north side of town, where thugs and hoodlums lined the streets in white tall tees and dreads. I rarely visited her, not because of the neighborhood, but because she preferred to come to me. My guess is that my place was like a vacation spot compared to hers. She didn't make a lot of money and wasn't the type to live beyond her means. Her new sedan was her most extravagant possession. San had plenty without having it all. I never once heard her complain.

Children were running barefoot in the streets of her apartment complex. Women were sitting on their porches doing hair, smoking cigarettes, talking on cordless house phones. San's car was parked outside but there were no lights on that were visible from the street. I parked near her car and ran up the stairs. The neighbors were attentive, admiring the red Mercedes I rented that week. By the second knock, the door was opened.

"What are you doing here?" She was wearing red boy shorts, a black halter that tied behind her neck and tube socks that almost reached her knees. She had her hair pinned up, off her shoulders.

Her eyes were puffy and her nose was red.

"I came to check on you. Are you sick or something?"

She examined herself, "No, I'm fine."

"It doesn't look that way to me, San. If you want me to leave I will, but don't lie to me."

"Come in." She stepped back to open the door just enough to let me in.

There were dishes stacked in the kitchen sink and paper scattered all over the living room floor. The air was damp, like cool air had not circulated through the space. She flung her body onto the sofa and tapped a box of cigarettes, relieving it of one. "Want one?" she motioned. I declined and sat next to her, wondering when she started smoking.

"Well, I'm still confused about what's going on here."

"I've been doing all I can to bring Sarai home. Everything."

"I know. You've been working hard."

"That's just it. The county has had a significant budget cut, and my job is out the window." She started to sort through some papers on the floor.

"You can get another job, San. What about something temporary?"

"No! I'm tired of this. I just want to be able to take care of my daughter and not keep scrounging around for employment."

"You will. I'll help you."

"So, is that it? You'll help me now. Everything is so damn easy for you. You need money; you do a show. You don't want to be bothered with someone; you don't answer your phone. I have to deal with my issues. I don't have easy resolutions."

I stood up, "I'll go." I refused to apologize for who I was and it was obviously not a good time to engage in an argument with her, so I didn't say anything.

"I won't ask you to stay, Taj." She looked up at me from the floor, holding the cigarette between her fingers pressed to her lips.

"Call me if you need me."

"Maybe then you'll decide to answer."

I had never felt sorry for her until that moment. Discovering that she had a weakness was momentous. I had searched all over her to find something that made us relatable. She finally became human in my sight, even attainable. It wasn't my intentions to prey on San's weakness, but only at that point did part of me want

Trickery

to give her everything she needed, her daughter, security. I felt helpless. For the first time, I didn't have an instant fix, but I would have done anything to help her. I walked down the concrete stairs quickly and rushed to my car. I opened the sunroof to let in some cool air then drove away.

Ten minutes into the drive from San's house I received a phone call.

"Hello," I answered. "What's wrong?"

"Nothing. You said to call if I needed you."

"Yeah?"

"I need you."

There was nothing that I could say. A sense of excitement rushed through me. She finally said what I regrettably feared to feel for her and I realized that I needed her just as much. It wasn't simply for sexual pleasure as it had been with others in the past, nor was it based on the fact that we shared a friendship, but because over time I had learned to trust, respect, and love her, a wonderful woman.

Trickery

Chapter Eight

Soon after the episode at San's apartment, she became my partner in crime, and a great one, might I add. I had not heard from Tiki in weeks, and a friend was in need of some fast cash. Of course I wouldn't refuse an opportunity to make some money, so I was all in.

San was dependable. She never stood me up or made excuses about why she couldn't work, even though she may not have been feeling well that day. She always wore a smile. It took her a while to get the idea that the show wasn't just a sexual encounter between two women, but a performance. She and I practiced role-playing on nights that we were not expected to perform. We practiced moaning and several movements that were more enticing, inviting. She mastered seductive lip biting and bedroom talk. I was turned on by listening most times.

Three months passed and we'd made enough money to last for at least six months. We relocated — together. I figured it would be helpful to the both of us if we were only responsible for half the bills. Our apartment was located on the south side of Jacksonville, near the beach. It was more expensive than either of us could afford without the other. There were three bedrooms, two and a half baths, granite countertops, glossy hardwood floors and a fireplace in both the living room and the master suite. It was a piece of art, which only increased in beauty when San added pieces she collected from a trip to Atlanta. My favorite painting was by artist Laurie Cooper. It was that of a woman, half darker-skinned with coarse hair and half lighter-skinned with gray eyes and straight hair. The imaged looked as though half of the face is peeling away, but which half the viewer cannot decide. She hung it over the mantelpiece, and it became the primary focus in our living room area.

For the most part, San and I shared the master suite. We hadn't declared to be in a committed relationship, but no title could have brought us any closer. We were truly partners in every aspect of our lives. There was a spare bedroom, fully furnished and decorated, in case one of us decided to move out of the master suite. The third bedroom held two twin-sized beds for the day that our children would be able to come and stay with us. That day came for San not long after moving into the new place.

"Guess what?" She came into the kitchen while I was chopping onions to add to a pot of browning ground beef.

"What?" I shifted to the oven, my back toward her.

"I'm going to Tampa tomorrow."

"Okay. It's not like you haven't been 20 times since I've known you."

"But wait! I'm bringing something back with me."

"Oh come on. No more knick-knacks from your mom's garage. If she didn't want it, I don't want it either. It's only going to collect dust just like —"

"No," she cut me off. "Maybe I should have said that I'm bringing someone back with me."

I gripped the spoon with which I was stirring the bubbling spaghetti sauce even tighter. Something prevented me from breathing properly and my vision became slightly blurred. I immediately knew who she was referring to. A part of me wanted to be happy for her. I couldn't be. Micah, my own son, still seemed so out of reach. After several inquiries, I hadn't received any phone calls or correspondence regarding his whereabouts. His foster parents had moved away, and there was no urgency to find him since the state believed he would be better off without me anyway. For a moment I reflected on the last time I saw him. That day, three different narcotics were running through my system.

52

Trickery

I was barely able to open my eyes, but he couldn't fathom the situation. He laughed and giggled on my knee until he was taken away a final time.

"Well, aren't you going to say anything?" she giggled, grabbing me from behind.

"That's nice. I'm happy for you." I didn't turn to look at her.

"Ahhh, is that all?" She positioned herself to be able to look me in the face. "What's wrong? Are you crying?"

"No, it's the onions. I think they got into my eyes or something." I grabbed a towel from the counter then wiped my face. "I really am happy that she is coming home, San. It's what you've been wanting for, for some time now."

"I know. I can't wait." She damn near skipped into the bedroom.

Four days later, she was there. She wasn't as I pictured her. I thought she would be the spitting image of San, light-skinned, pointy nose and big, beautiful eyes. She was the total opposite, but gorgeous nonetheless. Sarai was extremely soft-spoken and playful and would laugh at even the idea of something funny. She had her mother's intelligence though. She absorbed everything she viewed on television so San only allowed her to watch educational programs.

53

Trickery

Every other day San took Sarai on some outdoor adventure: to the park, the zoo, museum, toy stores and the beach. It was pleasing to watch the two of them together, but it only reminded me more of what was missing in my own life. It took weeks for me to learn to talk with Sarai. I'd kept my distance, but as time went by, she began to cling to me as though I were her other caregiver. Our favorite place was on the sofa in front of the television in the evenings. She would snuggle up close to me and watch old episodes of the "Fresh Prince of Bel-Air" or I would allow her to watch some cartoons on the big screen. We didn't become close enough for me to feel as though I was a motherly figure to her, but close enough for me to truly care about her.

Between San's time in front of the computer, writing her life away, her frequent Tampa visits and spending time with Sarai, we started to perform less and less. We weren't in dire need of money or anything, but I liked to keep stacking as much as I could just in case. We were down to performing once a week at one time, which was a major reduction compared to the four to five times a week that I was accustomed to. One night after leaving a performance, I decided to discuss our infrequent show situation with San as we loaded the truck with our belongings, preparing to go home for the night.

"So, how do you feel about me doing shows again with Tiki?" She ignored me, pretending not to hear anything I said. "Did you hear me?"

"Umm. You said something about Tiki. What was it?"

"The show. Would it be cool?"

She dropped her overnight bag into the trunk. "What do you think?"

"Well, I understand that you've gotten busy with writing and with Sarai and all. I know she's a handful. I just don't want to put any more pressure on you." My main concern wasn't San's lack of time or her priorities, but my own priorities and need for comfort.

"Yeah, thanks for being so considerate," she said sarcastically.

"What do you want me to do?" I asked, placing another bag in the trunk.

"Anything but a show with Tiki. That was the old you. Don't go back to that."

"No, that's where you're wrong. That's still me," I said in anger, upset by her remark.

"So, what? I'm not in this with you anymore?"

"No, that's not it. I just — I just want to be on the grind like we used to be, but I know you have other things going on, while there's nothing stopping me."

"Talk to me about it then. What's wrong with talking to me first?" She placed the final bag into the trunk, closed it then placed her hands on her hips.

"I am talking to you about it."

"No, you're not. You came to me with your own solution. A ridiculous solution, might I add."

"Well, I apologize for that, but the fact still remains that —."

"And what about Sarai? I don't want to do anything to lose her again."

"What? Doing this is what got her back to you. Are you serious?"

"Yeah, well, now that I have her, I don't want to mess it up."

"Then I need a new partner."

She climbed into the Lincoln Navigator, that week's rental,

Trickery

fastened her seatbelt, and placed her right hand on her forehead. She was silent for some time. I stared at her for a few seconds, thinking that it would trigger some sort of reaction, then buckled my own seatbelt and started the engine.

"I'll pick it up. We'll perform more," she compromised, not looking at me.

"Do you mean that, San?"

"Yeah, I mean it."

She didn't. We continued to perform one show a week, on nights that were most convenient for her. I complained and argued until my voice became raspy and my throat began to throb, but to no avail, she always got her way. It became a constant argument, week after week after week. I even threatened to not come home some nights. I never acted on it. My life had done a complete one-eighty. I was in love with a woman, living with her faithfully, caring for her daughter and hustling less because of her. I had lost control of my life, but a part of me found some solitude and happiness where I was, but constantly questioned how long I would remain there.

Trickery

Chapter Nine

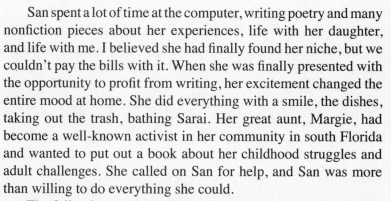

San spent a lot of time at the computer, writing poetry and many nonfiction pieces about her experiences, life with her daughter, and life with me. I believed she had finally found her niche, but we couldn't pay the bills with it. When she was finally presented with the opportunity to profit from writing, her excitement changed the entire mood at home. She did everything with a smile, the dishes, taking out the trash, bathing Sarai. Her great aunt, Margie, had become a well-known activist in her community in south Florida and wanted to put out a book about her childhood struggles and adult challenges. She called on San for help, and San was more than willing to do everything she could.

The following weekend San made plans to drive to Tampa for a face-to-face interview with her aunt. She packed very little the night before, just some jeans and cute tops, no make-up or heels. I finally believed in her cause.

"Are you gonna miss me?" She leaned in to kiss me.

"Maybe. Your side of the bed will be quite empty."

"Mm hm. Well, it should be." We both laughed. "Make sure you pick Sarai up from school today."

"How could I forget that?" I straightened the collar on

her shirt.

"All right, then I guess I better get going. I'll be back tomorrow night." She grabbed her bag, walked to the front door then turned for a final goodbye before she exited, "I love you."

"Yeah, me too. Drive carefully." She left.

I spent the remainder of the afternoon getting rid of clothes I hadn't worn in while so that I could hang up some of my new things. San's closet was nicely organized. She shopped less than I did, opting for an even higher quality, not quantity. I, on the other hand, liked a bit of both. The hours passed quickly and I figured I might as well pick up Sarai from school for her to spend the rest of the afternoon at home with me.

It had been four hours since San left and I hadn't heard anything from her. I attempted to call her twice en route to Sarai's school, but there was no answer. The drive would have only taken her about four hours, and San not answering my phone calls was extremely unlike her.

Time passed slowly waiting to hear from San. I managed to watch "Finding Nemo," two episodes of "Sponge Bob Square Pants," to play a few games of patty cake, and to sing a few old nursery rhymes when I realized it was almost 7:00 p.m. I hadn't received a phone call.

"Where's my mom?" Sarai asked as she combed the hair of her black Barbie. She sat next to me on the sofa with a few toys nearby in case she became bored with whatever she was watching on television.

"She'll be back — as soon as you wake up tomorrow." I stared blankly at the television.

"But I want — I want to see her," she whined.

"Not tonight, Sarai. Are you hungry?" I asked, hoping to distract her.

"Yeah. I want corndogs."

"Ok." I got up from the couch and went to the kitchen to prepare them.

I was placing the corn dogs in the oven when I faintly heard San's ring tone on my phone. I rushed over to the coffee table to grab it, trying hard not to alarm Sarai with my urgency.

"Hello? Hello?" I spoke quickly, walking into the bedroom and closing the door.

"Hey you," she said softly.

"Oh God. Tell me you're okay." I felt a sense of relief.

Trickery

"Yeah. I'm sorry I haven't called, but I realized that I left my cell phone charger at home. Look next to the bed. Is it there?"

I looked. It was plugged in the outlet next to the nightstand. "Yeah, it's there. You scared me."

"Well, I didn't want to waste my battery. I wanted to tell you goodnight. I'm really tired."

"Oh, okay, but Sarai wants to talk to you before —"

"No, I'll see her tomorrow. Give her a kiss for me okay. I'm about to —"

"Wait, she's right here and she really —" The phone went silent. "Hello, San? San?"

I'd never heard of her being too tired to even speak to Sarai. I rethought the conversation and realized how she failed to say she loved me. Then my mind became clouded with the thought of her being with someone else.

Who's there with her, I thought. What is she doing?

Then I remembered she'd left her jewelry, favorite perfumes, cosmetics and her sexiest lingerie. It also dawned on me that nothing could hinder her from buying new things if she wanted to. I refused to spend my entire evening wondering what was going on with her, like a vulnerable mess. I fed and bathed Sarai, then put her in bed, leaving the door to her room open slightly to reveal the light from the kitchen.

"Can I sleep with you?" she sat up in bed.

"No. You're a big girl."

"But I'm scared." She rubbed her eyes.

"Want me to keep your light on?" I flipped the switch, then stood in the doorway with my arms folded.

"No, I — I want to sleep with you." She looked at me sleepily, barely able to keep her eyes open.

"Come on." I turned off the light then followed her into our bedroom. She climbed into bed on San's side and got under the covers. I walked over to her and kissed her on the cheek as her mother instructed me and told her goodnight. She was asleep by the time I stepped out of the shower.

I didn't manage to fall asleep until 2:00 a.m. Sarai made her way to my side of the bed. Her features were so angelic, almost glowing. That night I saw her in a way I never had before. She was peaceful, innocent, just as her mother had been when we first met. I thought of Micah Anthony, my son. I wondered what he was doing, if he was sleeping as peacefully as Sarai, if he missed me as much as she missed her mother. I envisioned him lying there next to me. For an instant I could feel his breath on my shoulder, his foot pressed against my thigh, sense his warmth. Then the thought was gone.

The next morning I made breakfast for the both of us: scrambled eggs and cheese, biscuits, sausage and grits. It was more food than the two of us could finish, but we tried our hardest to stuff ourselves. Sarai lay down for a nap around noon while I cleaned the breakfast dishes from the morning. I stood over the sink, passing one dish at a time, from wash to rinse to dry, thinking of San and how she had not called at all that morning. I finished the dishes and went over to my phone to call her. As I dialed, I received an incoming call from an unfamiliar number.

"Hello?"

"Taj, girl, what's up?" She spoke quickly.

"Tiki?"

"Yeah, man, listen. I need a favor."

"What kind of favor?"

"I'm serious man. We can get paid." Her words ran together.

"For what, Tiki? What are you on? Why you talking so damn fast? I don't have time —"

"It's just for two hours San, please. You know the rapper, Lil T? Girl, anyway, him and his crew wanna see a show. And he really payin'. You know what I'm saying. Come on girl."

"Girl, I can't." There was silence.

"You know what — okay." The conversation became serious. "I never left your ass out to dry, did I? You know, I didn't even trip when you stopped our hustle. No one got money like us, Taj. Now when I really need you, you won't even take a moment to consider. I didn't know you were that damn cold!"

She rambled on for some time before I interceded. "All right. Where at?"

"What? You gon' do it?" She sounded surprised.

"Yeah, where? And how much?"

"Three Gs each. At the beach."

"All right. Two hours only. We have to do it around nine though. I can't be out too late."

"Okay, grandma. I hear you."

"See you later."

I knew I promised San that I wouldn't do any more shows with Tiki, but we're talking $3,000 in only two hours. I had already thought of ways to make it up to her. Although I felt guilty for leaving Tiki out in the cold in the first place, I didn't believe I owed my loyalty to either of them, so all was a go. I knew Tiki was able to get money on her own, but I knew that it wouldn't amount to the earning potential she had with me. San was due back home that evening, so I figured I would just go off once she arrived.

My thoughts were broken when I heard Sarai laughing at something on TV. I had no idea what was so funny, but I couldn't refrain from laughing. She danced around the apartment, sang, played with toys; we even went for a walk to a playground in the complex. I pushed her as high as I could on the swing, only for her to request to go higher. "I want to fly," she said.

"People can't fly, Sarai."

"Yeah they can. Keep pushing!" She giggled each time she went up.

"You can do whatever you want to do." I felt bad telling her that she couldn't do something.

"Yeah, I know. My mom told me." She let go of the chains and opened her arms as if she were flying. "I'm gonna fly. Make me fly, Taj."

"Oh no!" I grabbed the chains to the swing to slow it. "Don't do that! You'll fall and hurt yourself!"

"No, God will pick me up. Right?" She looked up at me. "He won't let me hurt, will He?"

I could not think of anything else to say. I'd never had a religious talk with a 4-year-old. "Who told you that?" I looked at her. "No. He won't," I said, realizing that it didn't matter where she'd learned it.

The day turned to night and we hadn't heard from San all day. I packed my things for the show, but I became nervous that there might be no one to watch Sarai, so I placed a few calls. Everyone was out of town, going out of town, working or had made plans. It was already half after eight and I had become desperate. The only other person I knew to call was Shai, and she agreed to watch Sarai.

With little help from me, Sarai put on her shoes. I brushed her hair and added a few barrettes. She went to her bedroom to get her favorite doll, the black Barbie with the Don King hairdo.

"No, leave that here." Barbie was holding on by an arm.

"Please, can I take her? I'll bring her back," she pleaded.

Trickery

"No, San hates when you take toys from the house." I took the toy from her and put it on the kitchen counter. "Come on, let's go."

She pouted.

Shai's house was only a 10-minute drive from the apartment, and when I pulled up to the driveway there were no other cars besides hers parked outside. Shai answered the door by the second time I rang the doorbell, wearing a forest green robe and smoking a cigarette.

"Girl, put that out before you kill yourself," I said, grabbing Sarai's hand to walk in the door.

"When it's my time, it's my time." She took one last puff and threw the cigarette into the grass. "Well aren't you a pretty little lady," she said, noticing Sarai standing beside me, "come on in here."

Shai's house was dark as usual, but there wasn't an enormous cloud of smoke or loud music blaring in any of the rooms. Sarai was calm. She sat on the sofa and laid her head on a throw pillow propped in its corner.

"Are you sleepy?" I caressed her face with the back of my hand.

"No. When is my mom coming?"

"You'll see her later."

"I want to go with you," she whined.

"No, I'll be right back. Aunt Shai is going to give you some cookies. You have to be a big girl if you want some cookies now."

"I know, but — but,"

"Be good. I'll be right back."

"You going to get my mom — to bring her home?"

"Yeah, I'm going to get her, but you have to be good."

She started to cry, struggling with the idea that I'd have to leave her there in order to bring her mom home to her, a catch-22. "Okay." She dried her face on the pillow.

"I'll be right back." I looked at Shai. "Keep an eye on her. She just likes to watch cartoons. She'll sit still."

"Girl, I got her. Go on."

Sarai sat up. She watched me walk away. I felt terrible for leaving her, but I knew I would see her in two hours.

It took another 15 minutes to get from Shai's house to the beach where I was performing that night. Getting out of my car, I could hear the waves crashing on shore and smell the salt of the ocean water. I couldn't think of anything more than making as much money as I could in that one night, then perhaps I may not have to work for a few weeks following.

Because of the thin walls, I could already hear music playing as I stepped off the elevator on the third floor. I even heard Tiki talking inside the room from the hallway. I knocked on the door, and when opened, a cloud of smoke rushed out into the hallway. The room was full of men, perhaps 15. There was barely any space to walk around. I spotted Tiki talking to one of the guys, but it wouldn't have served any justice calling her since she wouldn't have heard me over the music anyway. The guy she was talking to looked very familiar. He wore a plain, white T-shirt and a gray wash pair of Rock & Republic jeans. He had on minimal jewelry, only one ear was pierced and he wore a large-faced watch that glistened in the light.

Tiki looked different. It had been three months since I last saw her. She was thinner, but not a healthy thin. Her lingerie even fit loosely on her. And it wasn't like her to wear the same costume twice. I had seen that one many months before. I finally understood why she needed the money so badly.

"Hey you." I walked up from behind her.

"Heeeeyyyy!" She gave me a big drunken hug. "It's been a minute. You look good."

"So do you." I lied.

"Are you ready to get started?"

"Yeah, let me change first."

She pulled me into a corner by the arm. "No, we don't have time for that. These niggas ready to pay us. They don't give a damn about what you have on. You're already late. Let's get this money."

"So what am I supposed to do?" I noticed she was still gripping my arm, "and let me go!" I snatched my arm out of her grip.

"Play it off. We'll role play." I looked puzzled. "Just pretend like you just got home from work and I've been waiting. Then undress. You are wearing matching underwear, right?"

"Yeah, but —."

"Come on. Let's start."

She went over to the dresser and turned the music down. Tiki collected the money from Lil T first. I assumed she would lay down the rules as well since this was primarily her gig. Instead,

63

Trickery

she jumped into the bed and looked toward me to begin.

"Tiki, what about the rules?"

"Oh yeah, right." She propped up on her elbows, then said, "Oh, and anything goes!"

"What?"

"You heard me right. Girl, let's get this money," she whispered.

All eyes were on me. I couldn't just walk away. I dropped my bag and pulled my hair up from my shoulders and pinned it. I slowly unbuttoned my black and white polka dot blouse and removed it. The men were quiet. Tiki got on her hands and knees and slowly crawled over to me. She unbuttoned my pants and slid them down my thighs. My plum-colored, lace underwear was exposed for everyone to look at. I stood at the edge of the bed as she gripped my ass tightly and licked my panties like it were ice cream on a stick. I pulled them to the side, and the men leaned in for a better look. She made circles with her tongue. I climbed into bed on top of her, and we kissed passionately.

64

Trickery

I inched backwards on the bed to get into a position to go down on Tiki, ass raised in the air, exposing my goods. About a minute into the ordeal, I felt someone's hand on my thigh, making its way to my treasure.

"What the hell are you doing?"

"Chill baby." Some fool with more gold in his mouth than Mr. T's chains was standing behind me with a huge bulge in his pants.

"Oh hell no." I crawled back up to the top.

"It's ok. Just let me do you. Let me do you," Tiki said with a smile, making her way south.

For a moment it felt great. I never thought that I would miss having sex with Tiki, but I did. Although it was business, it was very pleasurable. It was only sex with Tiki; it was intimacy with San.

Tiki's body began to move back and forth, back and forth rhythmically, and she started to moan. I was in the middle of one of my "ooh" and "ahh" acting moments when I opened my eyes and looked toward the end of the bed. Tiki was being screwed from the back by Mr. Grillz, and he wasn't wearing a rubber. When he noticed that I was watching, he started to go harder and Tiki totally lost all control and focus. I kept my eyes on him, as I reached toward the floor for my shirt. I put it on, stood up, threw on my pants and grabbed my bag.

Lil' T grabbed my arm. "Where you going lil mama? The party just gettin' good."

"This not how I party though. I have to go."

"No you won't. Not until I get my money's worth."

"You can get plenty ass. You don't have to pay me for it. Let me go." I snatched away from him and left the room.

I didn't care about Tiki's safety in a room full of men. As far as I was concerned, she put herself in that predicament. I was so angry. During my drive to Shai's, I only wanted to get San on the phone and tell her all about it, but I knew it wasn't the right time to confess to what I had done that night. It was at that moment that my phone rang. I figured it would be Tiki, but it was San. I couldn't think of anything to say to her. Was she home? Had she been calling for a while? So many thoughts raced through my head before I had the courage to finally answer the phone before she went to voicemail.

"Hello?"

"Hey you. Are you sleeping?" I could hear the wind blowing through the window of her car.

"No. Where are you?"

"I'm getting on the road now. I should be there in about three hours."

"It's after ten o'clock, San. Why are you leaving so late?"

"Because I want to!"

I was shocked.

"What? Where'd that come from? What have you been doing? Who have you been with?" I questioned her forcefully.

"Let's not go there, Taj. I came to do what I said I would do. I just got caught up. That's all."

"Caught up with what? With who?"

"See, here we go. Every time —" San's voice was drowned out by sirens from a passing ambulance.

"I didn't hear you. Repeat that." A police car passed by, sirens echoed in the distance. "Don't worry about it. Even Sarai wanted to speak to you last night and you couldn't make time for her. What is this?"

"What are you trying to say, Taj? I'm not a good mother to my child?" She paused. "Sarai. Where is she?"

"She's —" Lights were flashing against Shai's house as I pulled onto her street. Three police cars and an ambulance were parked out front.

"What? I didn't hear you."

"Let me call you back."

"But wait! I was—"

"Let me call you back, San."

I don't remember hanging up or actually putting the phone down. I stared at each light as it lit up the scene, as if in a trance. I slowly got out of the car and closed the car door. I barely noticed the people to my left or my right. My vision was focused clearly on the front door of Shai's house. My first thought was that some fool has overdosed on some bad cocaine or ecstasy, and that it was my fault if Sarai had been exposed to it. I wanted to grab her, bring her out okay. I wanted to tuck her in that night like I had the night before, sit on the sofa and watch cartoons and play patty cake. The thought hit me hard and fast.

The front door was wide open, so I walked in. Shai was sitting on the couch where I had last seen Sarai, with a cigarette in her hand.

"Shai, what's going on?" She stared at the television. "Where is Sarai?"

She moved slowly. I assumed she was high. When her eyes finally met mine, I noticed one tear had made a path down her cheek. She spoke slowly, "Don't be — don't be mad at me."

"What?" I felt as though someone were stomping on my chest.

"She wanted to walk the puppy, and I told her 'yeah'. I say, 'stay away from that water out there. Don't go by that water.' She went by the water and —"

"She's four Shai! She can't walk a dog! Where is she?" I left Shai sitting on the sofa and ran to the back of the house. "Sarai? Sarai baby, come here." My limbs numbed and I became weak. The back door was open, so I walked through it. There was a gurney out by the lake. There was someone on it. "Oh God, no."

"No, no, no, no. Wait. No." A police officer grabbed my arms and held me from behind.

"Ma'am, we can't let you go over there. You understand?"

"No, no, wha — what — what's happened? Where is the girl? The girl? Please, God no."

"Ma'am, let's go inside so I can ask you some questions."

"Dammit! Let me go!"

"Ma'am, I'm not here to fight with you. I need you to calm

down and come with me. We're taking her to the hospital."

"Will she be okay?"

"Come with me."

He led me back into the house. I could barely walk or see through my clouded vision. My eyes were beginning to swell and I was getting hoarse. I sat on the sofa next to Shai.

"Ma'am, are you related to that girl?"

"No, I'm a friend of the family. I was watching her." His eyes were piercing. One of his bushy eyebrows was raised. His pale complexion contrasted with his dark facial hair.

"What's her name?"

"Sarai. Look, where are they taking her? I need to go." I stood up.

"Ma'am, have a seat." He motioned for me to sit down. "Where is her mother?"

"She's out of town. I mean, she's on the road — on the way back here."

"We'll need to contact the girl's mother."

"Will she be okay? Tell me dammit! What can I do?"

"I'm sorry to tell you this, but that little girl drowned back there in that lake. There wasn't anything any of us could have done to save her." I gasped for air. "Now, we need to contact her mother so that she's aware of what's going on here."

67

Trickery

I couldn't move. I plopped back down on the sofa. My hand landed on the damp pillow propped in its corner; the same pillow Sarai had laid her head and begged me not to leave her. My chest pounded faster with each second. My next move would be to lash out at Shai, strangle her, kick her, punch her, but she wasn't even worth the thought. She sat there, head titled back on the sofa, eyes barely open, unresponsive.

The lights outside began to dim as the rescue vehicles drove away. They had taken Sarai with them.

I grabbed my keys from the sofa and jetted for the door.

I couldn't sort through all the thoughts in my mind. I didn't want to call San. I was scared, hurt, frustrated. I was driving 20 miles over the speed limit, but I couldn't have cared less about a traffic ticket, which was minimal compared to my situation. I went back and forth about calling San the entire drive to the hospital. I thought about her being on the road, her safety. A part of me decided against it, even though I figured that if it were my child I would want to know immediately.

My hands trembled as I picked up the phone to call San, and having to do so invoked an even greater sadness. Although it was a clear night, my visibility was almost zero, so I pulled off the road. I sat there for five minutes, closing my eyes tightly, hoping that it was only a dream and I would soon wake up. It was still night, my eyes were still swollen, my throat still felt as though it were closing, there was no waking up from it. I finally pressed the call button on my phone. My heart pounded, breathing became painful; each exhale triggered a high pitch sound effect from somewhere within me. I pressed the phone to my ear. It went straight to voicemail. I was relieved for a moment, but it didn't take away what I felt about Sarai being gone.

They set her up in a room, in the dark. There was no one else there. I gave the nurses as much information on her as I could, then they closed the door and gave me a moment alone with her. The room was bare, only a bed and a stool, no equipment, an indication no attempts could be made to save her. There was a bright white light shining from above her bed. She seemed more angelic than the night before, peaceful.

Trickery

"Sarai." I walked over to the bed and softly touched her neck, one of her most ticklish spots. "Wake up baby. Laugh for me, please," I whispered. There was silence.

She was cold, her lips a shade of blue. I wanted to pick her up, shake her, take her home, and take care of her, play with her again. "Can you fly now? Did He catch you?"

I felt as though I carried myself from that hospital room. San had no clue what was going on and I wanted to be sure that I told her as soon as I possibly could. Out of anger my fast-talking, slick mouth had wished death on many people, but I wouldn't have ever wished something so horrific on Sarai.

Chapter Ten

The apartment was cold, extremely dark. I dropped my keys on the coffee table and turned on the kitchen light. On the counter, Sarai's Barbie laid naked, hair still out of whack. Something within me smiled, but again the thought of Sarai made me feel lower than I ever had before. I took the doll into the living room where I last played with Sarai, where we watched her favorite cartoons. It was quiet. I thought of going into the bedroom and packing my things. I figured that San wouldn't be able to live with me after she found out. Then I thought to go into the room and grab my bottle of Vicodin. I wondered how I could live with myself after what I had done. I opted for neither and just sat there.

Keys rattled outside the door. I couldn't look. San walked in with her bag and dropped it at the door. She didn't notice that I was there. Her keys clanked against the coffee table. She finally looked up and grabbed her chest.

"Dammit! You scared the hell out of me!" I didn't say a word. "Well, hey love. Why are you sitting out here?" She stood in front of me with her hands in the back pockets of her jeans. "Baby?"

I raised my head, "Yeah?"

"Are you upset about my phone, 'cause it went dead on the

way home. Fortunately, nothing happened for me to need my cell phone. You have to remind me not to forget these things," she said as she walked toward the kitchen.

I didn't say anything.

"Wow! That was a long drive. I don't think I want to do that again anytime soon." She opened the refrigerator, "And there are some crazy folks on the road too. What did you eat? Have you eaten?"

She walked back to the living room and stood in front of me again, her arms folded. "Taj, what's wrong with you? Why are you — ? Where is Sarai?"

I lowered my head and pressed both of my hands against my face.

"Sarai? Sarai?" she called. "Where is she, Taj?"

"Sit down, please." I mustered up enough courage to tell her.

"No! Tell me what's going on."

"SHE'S GONE!" I yelled. My nose was red, runny and throbbing.

"Where is she?"

"She died, San."

She laughed in disbelief, "No, no she didn't." Then she realized the state I was in and sensed my seriousness. She grabbed her throat. "What happened to my baby?"

"She drowned – in the lake – behind Shai's house."

"WHAT THE HELL WAS SHE DOING AT SHAI'S HOUSE, TAJ?"

"I can explain, but I don't think it's a good time to —"

"Oh God. You're serious." Her legs buckled and she fell to the floor. Her eyes were dry; she stared blankly. "And where is she now, Taj?" she whispered.

"The hospital — Shands. They put her in a room. She's —" San picked up her keys from the table and walked toward the door. I stood up. "I'm coming with you." I stood to leave with her.

"NO! NO!" She shoved me out of the way. "I don't want you to do or say anything to me right now! I'm going to get my baby," she began to sob.

I let her walk out, feeling undeserving to say another word.

"I'm sorry," I whispered to myself. "I'm sorry." I plopped down on the sofa, laid my head on its arm, and drifted off to sleep.

Trickery

Light was shining through the window when I finally awoke. My hair was disheveled, clothes wrinkled. I looked around the room. There was no one there. I went to the front door. It was still unlocked. San had not come back home. I checked my phone. No calls. I went into the bedroom, sat on the bed, and called the hospital.

"Shands Jacksonville. This is Pat. How can I help you?"

"Is Sarai Campbell still being held there?"

"Well, is she an admitted patient? Or is she in the ER?"

"She died last night and was being held there."

"Ok. Hold on a moment please." She placed me on hold. Music played in the headset. "There is no one here by that name, ma'am."

"Well, when did they remove her? And where did they take her?"

"I'm not permitted to share that information with you." My face tightened.

"What do you mean? My name is Taj Jenson. I was there when she arrived."

"I'm sorry ma'am. Is there anything else that I can help you with?"

"Yes, you can tell me where she is!"

"I'm sorry ma'am. I can't help you." She hung up.

I sat there looking at the phone, confused. Perhaps it was all a dream after all. I jumped up from the bed, went into the living room and took a look around. Everything was in place, like any other day that San would go off to write in the local coffee shop and drop Sarai off to school. There was something on the floor beneath the coffee table. I walked over and picked it up. It was Sarai's Barbie. I had fallen asleep with it the night before — the night Sarai died.

The hot water from the shower was soothing as I tried my hardest to recount the events of the previous evening. I felt like I was trapped in a horror movie, or that someone was playing some kind of sick prank on me. The bed looked more inviting than ever, so I climbed in, threw the sheets over my head, and wept. With each cry, spasms moved through every internal organ, forcing my abdominals to contract, my biceps to tighten. I wondered what would happen with San and me. Would she leave me now? Would

71

Trickery

I go back to life without her? I hadn't answered why Sarai was at Shai's house in the first place, and I wasn't prepared to tell her. It would only make the situation worse.

72

Trickery

Chapter Eleven

Tiki called at least twice a day, seven days a week for a while following the show, leaving messages threatening to kill me when she saw me again for the stunt I pulled. I disregarded each of her threats and refused to answer calls from unfamiliar numbers.

I didn't hear from San for a while, but kept track of her by monthly bank statements that were mailed to the apartment, which indicated that she was spending minimally in Tampa. She had gone back to be with her family. I thought she would never return until she resurfaced two months later. When San came home, she refused to talk about anything that went on that night. I had many questions that went unanswered: What happened with Sarai? Why wasn't I notified of funeral arrangements? What had she been up to during her time away? I was curious, but so remorseful about what I had done that I didn't want to force anything out of her. San was extremely quiet most times and never smiled or became excited about anything. I remember a time when she would write poetry or short stories, she would be so proud of that she'd beg me to read them only moments after they were written. After her return, she would only sit in front of the computer, typing away until she'd fall asleep, cheek pressed against the keyboard.

San took up the space in the guest room. We barely spoke, only to ask if one was hungry or not. The routine went on for three weeks. We were strangers forced to live under one roof. We were no longer friends, no longer partners. There was no love there. I felt so undeserving of her presence that I quickly forced myself to adjust to our awkward behavior. From time to time I would send flowers to our apartment with messages handwritten on tiny cards. The flowers would be left on the counter with the unopened envelope. The void resurfaced.

One night, while watching television in the living room, I received a phone call from a new associate, someone I had performed for with San months earlier. He invited me to a local jazz spot downtown, and I was anxious to get out of the house for the evening. I thought to invite San, but I didn't, fearing I would be rejected. I rushed off to the shower to prepare.

I wore a gray and white halter dress that I had purchased from BeBe weeks before. I squirted on a bit of DKNY Be Delicious perfume, only a corner remained in the bottle, swept my hair up into a nice tight bun, revealing more subtle sensual aspects of my body, my neck, shoulders.

Trickery

I needed to call for directions and realized I had left my cell phone on the coffee table in the living room. I opened the bedroom door slowly then walked out of the room. I noticed my cell phone on the coffee table. It was lit. At first I figured that someone had called. No one had. Then I checked my messages. None of those either. I looked at San whose back was toward me. She was staring at the computer screen, sitting silently. Has she gone through my phone? I thought.

I looked through some of my messages and previous phone calls. Some were to old friends, many to my new friend. I was nervous about what she may have learned if she had gone through old text messages from him. I couldn't show that I was bothered by what I assumed was a situation, so I grabbed my bag and my keys then walked out the front door.

We spent the evening laughing, talking, and enjoying the live band that played oldies like Johnny Gill's "My, My, My" and Jill Scott's "He Loves Me" while vocalists sang the old tunes. His name was Carl, half black, half something else that I never asked about. His hair was a different grade, slick and shiny. He had almond-shaped eyes and an imperfect smile that appealed most to me. Carl was a Navy corpsman, stationed at Mayport in Jacksonville. I found myself attracted to him, but then again, anything would have been attractive outside of my situation at home. We ended our night with a hug and a goodbye. I wasn't ready to stop smiling, laughing.

It was a quarter after one when I arrived home. There was no sign of San. There was still one surviving bouquet of flowers remaining on the counter. The note card was no longer attached. "San?" I called out. There was no answer. I figured that she must have left or was asleep, so I went to the bedroom to get undressed.

There was light flickering beneath my bedroom door. I opened it slowly, and there was San, lying on her old side of the bed with a candle on the nightstand next to her. She was sleeping. What is she doing in here? I thought. She appeared peaceful, angelic, nestled comfortably under the feather-stuffed down comforter. I didn't wake her. I stepped out of my dress and lay in the bed beside her. She rolled over, turned toward me, and put one arm over my shoulder and held me tightly. I fell asleep.

"Hey you," she whispered. Light was shining through the bedroom window. She was lying on my chest, propped on her forearm.

Trickery

"Yeah?" I said sleepily.

"Want breakfast?"

"Um, yeah, sure."

She jumped out of bed and went to the kitchen. I could hear pots and pans colliding with one other and didn't know what to make of the situation. I figured that this was better than silence, so I went along with it. I showered and slipped on a robe. Stepping out of the bedroom, I could distinctively smell the bacon, biscuits and the cheese eggs being scrambled on the stove. San turned from the stove and smirked. I returned her gesture with a friendly "hello" and sat down on a bar stool where she had placed champagne flutes filled with orange juice.

"How was your evening?" she asked.

"Fine." I was holding back.

"I guess that's good."

"Is there something you want to talk about, San?" I asked, hoping that she was ready to talk about Sarai, but fearing that she would question me about the night before.

"Yes, there is." She scraped the eggs onto a plate next to the stove.

"Ok, what's that?"

She moved the plates to the counter in front of me then rested her hands on the sink. "I want to move."

"To where?"

"Away from here. Atlanta maybe, even Houston."

"Why so far away? Why not Tampa, where your entire family is?"

"They're not my family." I looked serious. "And I can't stand being here anymore. I'm constantly reminded of — of the past. I think it would do us both good if we just packed up and left next week."

I almost choked on the biscuit I had stuffed into my mouth. "Next week?"

"Yeah. This place is already paid for. We have money in savings and we could always make more if we needed it." She made her way around the bar to sit next to me. "What do you think?"

"Um, I'll have to think about it."

There was no doubt in my mind that I would even consider leaving Jacksonville. The entire situation was extremely odd. We hadn't spoken for months and all of a sudden she's ready to pack up and leave with me.

"I have a way for us to make five grand."

"What?" I was really curious. "In one night?"

"Yeah, there are some guys that want a private show. They got a lot of —"

I thought about the last show I did with Tiki and refused to go through it again. "No, I can't."

"But why? Let's just make the money, get out of town, and start over."

"Maybe I don't want to start over, San."

"Don't be so selfish."

"I don't have time for this," I said under my breath and left the room.

She never brought it up again. We both understood that in time our funds would be depleted and we needed to make more money, so we began doing shows again, starting with only five to six men in one sitting, then increasing to our typical 12 to 14 attendees. There was no longer any passion or excitement in our performances. We were acting, completely. The only improvement that occurred within the home was that we were finally communicating about some things, but for the most part remained distant from each other.

It was December, a week before Christmas, and San and I planned one last show before the holidays, which we planned to spend in New York that year, a place she had never been. The show was to be held at a hotel on the south side of town. San informed me that she'd arranged for 12 guests to show up that night. It was the first time she had taken full control of a show. I prepared as I usually had, but San did not. She showered at home and wore her lingerie beneath jeans and a t-shirt. When I asked why she was preparing at home, she said it was more comfortable, convenient, and that she was tired of lugging all of the bags to the car at the end of the night.

We arrived at the hotel two hours before the show was set to begin, so after I was dressed we lay across the bed and expressed how excited we both were about our trip to New York. We talked about visiting Times Square, watching a play on Broadway and shopping in Harlem and on Fifth Avenue. She made me smile again for the first time. For a moment there was that old energy between us that was there in the beginning. I played in her hair, twisting her locks while she was lying on her back. She caressed my shoulder with her fingertips. We laughed together.

Trickery

There was a knock on the door and San and I jumped up from our relaxed positions in bed. I sat up, back pressed against the headboard, legs crossed, while San went to the door. She turned to look at me before she opened the door, making sure I was ready.

"Heeyyyy!" San reached up to hug the men walking through the door.

"Hey girl. You looking good." He had to be about 6-foot-4, 245 pounds, all muscle. He was darker skinned, very clean-cut, and was wearing a pair of Rock & Republic jeans and a blue collared shirt he probably picked up at Express.

The other guy looked more serious. He hugged San without saying anything. He wasn't as big, 6-foot maybe, 190. He had on a pair of basketball shorts, a t-shirt, and could have used a good shave.

"Hey, you must be Taj." The clean-cut guy reached over the bed to hug me.

"Yeah. What's your name?"

"Leon." He smelled sweet.

"Well, it's nice to meet you, Leon." I flirted. "Who is

your friend?"

"Um, that's my boy, Tony."

"Does he talk?" I said loud enough for him to hear me. He was sitting in a chair on the opposite side of the room.

"Yeah, I talk," was all he said. His voice caused me to tremble a bit, very deep.

Leon talked with me for a while, and San entertained Tony. I was expecting at least 10 others and it was almost a half hour after the show was set to begin. I excused myself from our conversation about Jacksonville's new developing communities and went over to San.

"Where is everyone?"

"I don't know. I had confirmation."

"Are you sure?" She nodded her head. "We can't do it with just these two."

Tony looked directly at me, "Why not?"

"I'm not talking to you."

"Probably not, but you're going to give me what I came here for. This already paid for."

"We haven't collected any money from you yet."

"Like hell you didn't. I gave ol' girl over two stacks."

I looked at San who was staring off in another direction but could clearly hear the conversation. "What did you buy for two stacks?" I felt butterflies, not the good ones.

"A good time." He smirked.

I grabbed San's arm and started toward the bathroom. Tony jumped up to block our way, arms extended.

"What are you doing?" I squeezed San's arm tighter. She didn't say anything.

"Come on. I get one hour, right?" San nodded her head but remained silent. I finally understood what was going on. This was San's plan to get us out of town. I let her go and backed away from them. I noticed that Leon was standing near the bed, observing, arms folded.

"Taj, I can't give their money back. I can't," she said, remorsefully.

I looked toward the front door, at the three of them, then the front door again. The dresser was behind me, holding bottles of liquor we'd bought for that evening. The balcony was on the opposite side, closed and locked.

I grabbed a half-empty bottle of Grey Goose then charged at

Tony. I hit him as hard as I could and ran toward the door. The bottle didn't break; it only made a loud thumping noise. He fell to the floor. I couldn't remove the latch at the top of the door fast enough to open it before Leon grabbed me from behind and threw me near the bed. San disappeared. Tony stood up slowly, holding his ear, "DAMN! You stupid bitch!"

"I'll give your money back. Just let me get it," I pleaded.

He walked over and slapped me with the back of his hand. My body lay stretched over the bed. I attempted to crawl to the phone. He pulled me back by the ankle.

"Please, don't hit me any —" His fist collided with my jawbone. I felt a snap, a burning sensation, warm fluid oozing from my flesh. My mouth had become too impaired to speak, or yell. He didn't stop there. Each blow delivered pain on contact; a severe tingling in one eye, then the other, blood gushing through my nose made it impossible to breathe; there was that drowning sensation in my nose and throat, I was suffocating. He vocalized every blow he delivered to my body, but his sounds were soon overpowered by ringing in my ears. I lay there, silently praying for him to stop — for him to become so tired he'd quit, but when he did, he no longer hit me with his hands. I couldn't make out what the object was, but it was as solid and hit as hard as a baseball bat, delivering instant agony to my head, abdomen, and chest, until after a while I was no longer able to see, or hear, or speak, or move. I could barely breathe, let alone put forth the energy to cry through the beating. And after a while longer I felt no more pain as I slipped into a state of unconsciousness.

There was a moment that I can recall waking up in the middle of the ordeal. I was lying face down across the bed, the lower half of my body unsupported by the mattress. I was being penetrated, deep inside. Each movement was like sandpaper entering and exiting my walls. In the darkness behind my swollen lids, I wailed as loud as I could. I couldn't feel the moistness of tears on my cheeks, but they had to have been there. I tried to block it out of mind, but the pain was unbearable. My knee-jerk reaction was to stop him. With my left arm I reached behind in attempt to push him away. He grabbed and twisted it, pinning it against my body. I attempted to scream out, but was gagged with my own blood instead. And then, I caught a glimpse of her, San, standing in the corner of the room, arms folded, watching as though she were a guest viewing the show. Then, I went unconscious again.

Chapter Twelve

There was a series of beeps echoing for what felt like an hour before I completely opened my eyes. It became obvious that I was in a hospital room. The sheets were white and crisp; there was an IV machine next to the bed along with other equipment that created the beeps that resonated in my mind. I couldn't feel anything beyond the aching throughout my torso. I felt heavy, swollen. Wiggling my fingers was painful. I believed my left arm was broken, so I explored my body with my right hand; some parts were more swollen than others. .

I could recall the events that led me to the hospital, but I had no memory of how I had gotten there. It remained difficult to see through my swollen eyes but, needless to say, they were better than they had been. My left arm was in a cast, resting on my chest. My neck was incredibly stiff.

"Somebody," I whispered with a voice low and raspy. "Somebody, please."

No one came. No one heard me. I drifted back to sleep.

"And what's her story?" a female voice asked.

"We don't know yet, but she's better than she was when she got here."

"Well, of course, she has the best doctor in the city," she flirted.

I couldn't open my eyes fast enough, heavily under the influence of whatever was in my IV.

"If you say so." I heard the door open and close again. "Who could have done this to such a pretty girl?" The male voice spoke again. I could hear his pen pressing hard against whatever he was writing on. He hummed Luther Vandross' "If This World Were Mine" and remained in the room for only a moment, then was gone.

After he left, I mustered enough strength to open my eyes completely and sit up in bed. There was a cup of grape juice and a cup of yogurt next to the bed. I drank two gulps of juice then examined the room. I was alone, somewhere. I looked at the telephone. The receiver read: St. Vincent's Medical Center.

The door opened.

"Someone's awake." It was a white female with dark brown, shoulder-length hair, wearing blue medical scrubs. She came over to the bed and checked my IV. "How are you feeling?"

I looked at her through the small openings I had for my eyes. "I'm okay."

"I'm going to send Dr. Carter in to have a look at you since you're awake."

"Ok. Can I ask you a question?" I asked in a whisper. "How did I get here?"

"You can ask the doctor about that." She turned to leave.

"Thank you."

The clock on the wall indicated it was after 8:30. I could only assume that it was night because no sun reflected through the windows at the rear of the room. I had to have been there for at least 16 hours. I thought about leaving, recounting the previous night's events, wondering where the hell San was and how I was going to mess her up when I saw her again. My pain turned to anger, especially while thinking that they could have permanently scarred my face, my most valuable asset.

A man wearing jeans and a collared shirt walked into the

room. He was fairly handsome, tall, in great shape. I noticed his biceps before his face, which topped it off. He looked serious.

"How are you feeling?" He closed the door behind himself.

"Are you the doctor?"

"Yes, I am. I'm sorry about my attire. I was heading out to meet some friends and heard that you were awake."

"I just wanted to be sure strangers weren't just coming in to ask my personal business."

"I understand that." He looked over the charts.

"I'm feeling fine though. Can I sign out now?"

"Nooo, no, you can't. We need to talk about a few things first." He pulled up a small, rolling stool and sat near the bed.

"I don't want to talk about anything. I really think I'll feel better if I just went home. I hate hospitals."

"You can start by telling me your name," he said, ignoring everything I had told him.

"Taj Jenson," I replied, annoyed.

"Do you have any close relatives that we may contact? – with your permission, of course."

"No." There was an awkward silence. "Are you going to just tell me what's wrong with me, or am I going to be here for another hour while you rack up on a huge medical bill? Hasn't it been over 12 hours already? This is ridiculous."

"Calm down please. You've been in here for two days, not hours." My eyes widened. "You suffered a concussion, a lot of bruising and swelling; your left arm is broken in two places, and you —" he paused for a moment. "When was the last time you had intercourse?"

"A while ago. Why?"

"I'm sorry to tell you this, but there is a lot of bruising and swelling in your vaginal area." I looked to the ceiling.

"Ok, whatever. When can I leave?" I knew there would be a series of questions following, and I wasn't going to answer them.

"Ms. Jenson, you were raped and I can't imagine how you may be feeling right now, but you need to speak with the officers who can help you with this."

"No. I don't need to do anything. Can you just sign the paper so I can get out of here? Forget it; you don't need to sign anything. This is a free country and I'm —"

"Not going anywhere. Listen, I don't want you to make a decision that may jeopardize your health, so I'll put contacting the authorities to let them know that you're awake on hold for a moment. Promise me you won't disappear in the middle of the night."

"No cops?"

"I'll have them on speed-dial if you want to talk, but I won't contact them without your permission." I folded my arms. "No, no cops. Get some sleep. We'll talk about this more in the morning." He checked the IV. "Are you comfortable? Hungry?"

"Yeah. I haven't eaten in a while."

"I'll have the nurse send for something that you'll be able to chew in your condition." He grabbed my right hand. "Goodnight."

Before he walked out, I said "Thank you". He nodded his head and was on his way.

I hadn't considered the fact that I was involved in a crime, the fact that my blood was smeared over hotel room sheets and that my body was found beaten and unconscious in a public place. That hadn't clicked until the moment Dr. Carter came into my room. There was no way I was going to speak with authorities about the incident. We weren't supposed to be there in the first place. How could I explain that this was just a good-deal-gone-bad and that my supposed girlfriend set me up? I was expecting for the finger to be pointed back at me. The situation would be reminiscent of my childhood, where I was to blame for everything in spite of being the victim. How would I know for sure that I wouldn't be arrested for my part that evening, arranging for men to pay me to perform a public sex act? That was the problem. I had my life, so everything else had to be buried in the past.

Trickery

My first objective was to get out of bed, a task that would take me almost an hour to achieve alone. My body seemed detached from some central system holding everything together. The swelling had decreased significantly, but parts of my body still remained sore, bruised. The first time I confronted a mirror, I hardly noticed the person behind the black and blue blotches that covered my face. Everything was intact, just temporarily damaged, nothing I couldn't recover from with the help of pure cocoa and shea butters. My lip was healing well, and so was the inside of my jaws. I had been weaned off of heavy medication, but doctors were still monitoring my progress.

Two more days passed in the hospital when Dr. Carter realized no one was coming to visit me, so he checked on me more often than he should have. Once, he brought me an arrangement of fresh flowers and a teddy bear that read "Get Well Soon". He was friendly, sometimes too friendly, asking me about personal relationships and family, but when his questions were ignored, he'd change the subject, fearing he was crossing the line. I saw him as this ordinary, borderline goofy guy who made a slick attempt to get close to me. I admired his physique in many ways but his personality was barely up to par. I sensed power behind that doctor's coat, which was his most attractive quality.

"They're letting you go home today." He stared at the chart he was holding, facing away from me.

"Well, don't be too happy about it," I said sarcastically. I sat at the edge of the bed, fully dressed in a shirt with a colorful map of Florida printed on the front and some blue gym shorts I'd purchased in the hospital's gift shop.

"I'm happy that you're well enough to go home, but I still have some concerns about your well-being, you know, what landed you here in the first place. I don't want to see you here again, not in that way."

"In some other way, perhaps?" I giggled.

"Maybe. I just want you to be careful, and if there is anything you may need in the future, you know where to find me. Okay?"

"Okay."

Dr. Carter prescribed some medications, explained the dosages and handed me a few other sheets of paper as well as a plastic bag that contained a set of keys, some lip gloss, and a pair of earrings that were gathered from the room before the ambulance transported me. He advised me to return in two weeks for him to check the progress of the broken arm. In all, I spent five days in the hospital recovering from the beating. I was still not operating at one hundred percent, but was able to care for myself without the help of others and with hope that the remainder of my scars, wounds, and pains would vanish as quickly as others had.

"And who's coming to get you, Taj?"

I was silent, realizing the thought hadn't crossed my mind up to that point. I contemplated calling a taxi, which led to the thought that I needed money, then to the idea that I had no wallet, no cash, and no cards.

"I'll call someone," I said.

"Okay, just keep in mind what I told you." He reached out to shake my hand. I sensed that he would rather have a hug by how deeply he stared into my eyes and firmly gripped my hand, slightly pulling me toward him.

"Thank you for all your help. I will." He walked out of my room for the last time.

Where was I going to find money to pay for a ride home? Where was home? Was San still there? So many thoughts clouded my mind when I was released. A part of me felt safe and comfortable in a hospital bed with people catering to my needs. It was time to go, so I had no choice but to face whatever else was ahead of me. I used the phone next to the bed to dial the credit union where San and I kept our savings from performances. The account had been emptied; only three dollars and eighteen cents remained. At one point, there had been more than twelve thousand dollars in the account. She had cleaned it out completely. I couldn't panic and let everyone else know that something was wrong. I simply inquired about public transportation, and a lady at the nurses' station arranged for someone to take me home.

Silently, I said goodbye to my hospital bed, the room, the staff, and the building itself as I stepped onto the van. There were two older women aboard, one man. I told the driver my address, found a seat at the back, and stared from the window the entire way home. No one spoke. One by one, the driver let off each passenger. It took over an hour before we reached my place of residence.

"Is this your stop?" he called.

"Yeah, this is fine."

I noticed the Jaguar that I rented the week before was still parked in the lot. The sun was completely hidden, but I didn't notice any lights on inside the apartment. I pictured San being there, wanting to harm me even more, but then I figured that nothing could hurt as bad as the initial beating, or as bad as the betrayal I felt.

I reached into the bag for the set of keys but noticed that the door was cracked open. I peered through the tiny slit in the door, darkness. There wasn't any movement, no sound. I pushed the door open with my cast. "Hello?" I called out, hoping no one would answer. There was no longer any furniture in the space, even the Laurie Cooper painting had been removed; only the nails remained. There was no television, sofa, tables or lamps. It seemed as though, in a hurry, they had broken a vase that held fresh-cut flowers on what used to be an end table next to the sofa, not having time to clean up the mess. There were still indentations

Trickery

in the carpet where furniture had been.

No clothes were left hanging in my closet, only underwear, folded t-shirts, what I called "house clothes". My bed was still there, stripped of the jacquard comforter set I had purchased from Macy's a week before. Sarai's old bedroom was intact; nothing was taken. I returned to my bedroom after evaluating the apartment, sat on the edge of the bed, observed my surroundings while scratching at the cast on my left arm, making a zipping sound. I hummed some made-up tune in the dark, legs swinging from the edge of the bed, still scratching at my cast, regretting every moment I'd spent with San, the day I met her, how much I'd let her in. It was Christmas Eve.

Trickery

Chapter Thirteen

I no longer had a cell phone. It was left back at the hotel room if San hadn't taken that too, and I had no intentions of retrieving it. I desired darkness, rest, and sleep, something I'd never wanted so much of before. Each day, I recounted the events of that evening, the feeling of being pounded numb, the look on San's face, her failure to help me, the idea that I could have died. With only $1,600 that was stuffed in the Jaguar's glove compartment, I thought of what I would do next, if I was going to move away, or ever work again. For the time being, there was nowhere else for me to go so I had the locks changed in case someone decided to come around looking for trouble.

My appointment with Dr. Carter was held on a Wednesday. By then, most of my scarring was minimal. A good liquid foundation covered what remained. I was thankful for how well Dr. Carter treated me while in his care. Because of him, I didn't mind that I had no one else to come and check in on me. He was so compassionate, and I was sure to thank him when I saw him again.

I curled my hair in loose spirals and fingered the curls apart for a softer look. I wore a blue blouse by Chanel that revealed most of my back with its deep V-cut and a pair of Dior jeans, all of which was in the laundry when San cleared the house. I stood in the mirror for almost an hour, making sure that each imperfection on my face was covered perfectly, yet subtly. It was the first time I had dressed up since that night.

The Jaguar was returned to the rental company, so I called a taxi, a sixty-dollar-round-trip ride across town. I walked into the hospital, took the elevator to the fourth floor, and approached a receptionist who was completing a sudoku puzzle.

I placed my left arm with the cast on the counter and asked, "Is Dr. Carter here? I have an appointment."

"And your name?" she said with an attitude, as though I was interrupting her.

"Taj Jenson." She looked at the computer screen.

"Ok. Sign there and have a seat." She went back to the puzzle.

I sat across from a little girl holding a black, anorexic-looking doll. Her mother wasn't paying her too much attention — preoccupied by her telephone conversation. The little girl wouldn't look away. She stared directly at me. I picked up a copy of the Cosmopolitan from the coffee table — How to Make Him Crave You stretched across the cover. I turned each page anxiously, knowing that at any moment Dr. Carter would come out to greet me. I waited for 15 minutes before a young, Hispanic woman wearing scrubs appeared in the doorway and called my name.

Trickery

"Yes," I responded.

"Come with me. I'll take you back." I followed her down a long, empty hallway past several closed doors. "You can wait in here until he comes in."

"Thank you." I walked into the room, placed my Burberry bag on the leather swivel stool next to the counter then sat on the bed. Before I was able to get comfortable, he walked into the room wearing a white lab coat and khaki-colored pants.

"Ms. Jenson, how are you?" He reached out to shake my hand.

"I've been well. Just taking some time to heal and take care of myself, you know."

"And as far as I can see, you're doing a wonderful job. You look — umm — great."

"What was the umm all about?"

"It's difficult to compliment such a gorgeous lady while I'm working. I should have arranged for you to see another doctor to make this less awkward, but I figured I'd take the risk." He laughed.

"Well, I would have insisted on seeing you, Dr. Carter." I giggled. There was no denying some sort of attraction.

"You know, you won't have to see me after today, so I'd prefer that you call me James. It's my first name."

"James Carter." I said, as if I didn't already know it.

The remainder of the visit went as planned. The cast was removed from my arm and everything else seemed to check out fine. In between procedures, Dr. Carter and I managed to comment on politics and the failing education system. He was more intriguing, knowledgeable and sophisticated than I originally thought.

That evening, once I arrived home, I called him at a phone number listed on his business card from a prepaid phone I had picked up at the local Walmart. It eventually went to voicemail.

"Hey James. It's me, Taj." I said seductively. "It was really nice seeing you today. Maybe we can have dinner soon. Be sure to call me back. Bye."

Trickery

Within the hour he had returned the phone call and made plans to meet me for a late Thursday night dinner. I saw it as an opportunity to finally impress him outside of the office.

For some odd reason, I expected dinner at the local TGI Fridays, Chili's or Ruby Tuesday, and at most a visit to the local Japanese hibachi grill. He took me downtown. The blue neon light over the bridge shimmered over the St. John's River as we crossed. Morton's had been a spot that he frequented, where he said we could find the freshest seafood and the best steaks. I had thought only I was accustomed to fine dining, up until that point anyway.

We pulled up to valet and James left the keys in the ignition and climbed out to open the door of his black, late modeled Range Rover for me. The cool breeze lifted the scent of Amor Amor from my sweet spots and filled the surrounding air. I stepped out of the car one blue suede BCBG stiletto sling back at a time and grabbed his hand to enter the restaurant.

We dined on colossal shrimp, lobster, and sea bass, along with two glasses of the restaurant's best Riesling, which was then followed by a deep conversation in which he revealed a previous failed marriage and his struggle to move on from it. He never revealed specifics, only mentioning that his ex-wife was "selfish in every way imaginable" and that "he's happier now than he's ever been." I imagined ways to make him happier. James was someone that I had become curious about, and was not simply an object to be conquered and devoured as I had with other men.

"How was your dinner?" he asked, placing his wine glass back on the table after a sip.

"It was really good. The mango salsa on the sea bass totally made the dish. How was yours?" I looked over to his plate. He had barely eaten anything.

"It's great. I don't have too much of an appetite this evening. I guess my mind is a little preoccupied."

"Would you like to share?" I offered.

"I already am." He lifted his glass again. I blushed and lowered my head, then removed my napkin from my lap and laid it on the table. "Are you ready to leave?"

"Whenever you are." I folded my hands in front of me and rested my jaw on the knuckles.

"You're beautiful." He paused. "I mean, I know you hear it quite often, but you're gorgeous beyond your physical beauty. As cliché as it sounds, there is just something about you."

92

Trickery

I smiled. "Well, wait 'til you've known me for a month. You'll be dying to get rid of me." We both laughed. He paid the tab and we left the dining room area, but not before I stopped by the ladies room to check my make-up and add a dab of perfume to freshen up.

James was putting on his coat and draping a heavy scarf around him, a bit much for a Florida winter, but the act was something like I'd never seen before. He exuded power and dominance, yet revealed a more sensitive side through his conversations and interactions with me. How could this man be single, I thought.

Heat blasted from the air vents when we got into the car, the valet's method of warming it up before handing it over. He decreased the level of airflow then reached over and grabbed my hand.

"Where to ma'am?" he smirked.

"Perhaps you won't mind takin' me 'round to the Piggly Wiggly." We both laughed. "I wouldn't consider myself the average Ms. Daisy, so why don't we try that again."

He chuckled a little. "Is there anywhere that you would like to go?"

"No. It's cold out, and I've had a long night. I think it's time that I turned in."

"Do you have to get up early? Wait, what is it that you do?" He raised an eyebrow.

Damn! I forgot to come up with something beforehand. I was completely caught off guard. "A little bit of this, a little of that. I work in the entertainment industry — you know, promoting, booking, and modeling — a bit of everything." I stared through the windshield, not wanting to read an expression on his face, but for some reason I could tell he knew I wasn't being truthful.

"Well, I'll get you home so you can get some rest. Tomorrow is my only day off this week unless I get a call. I would love to spend more time with you this evening though."

"No, but thank you. It's really not a good time. I had a great time with you tonight." I knew that if I gave in and became too available my relationship with him would have been shortened. A few sips of wine and flirting would most definitely lead to sex, causing my value to depreciate at least 60 percent.

"It's cool. Maybe we can meet up next week some time if you're not too busy." I knew he was being sarcastic. How could anything that I have to do compare to his position as a physician, but I didn't say anything. It was a horrible lie that totally lacked creativity.

Trickery

He dropped me off in the dark, desolate lot of my complex. He didn't bother to get out, but leaned across the seat and slowly pressed his succulent lips against mine.

"Thanks again for everything."

"I'll call you tomorrow. You have a good night." He checked the back seat to make sure I wasn't leaving anything behind.

"I think I have everything. Goodnight."

I walked to the door and let myself in. I could hear my movements echoing through the empty apartment. The air was cold and it was extremely dark. I reached over to turn on the light, but it wouldn't come on. I figured that the bulb had blown at some point, so I tried another switch near the bedroom. No luck. The power was out and it was near freezing outside.

In the darkness I went for an old pair of sweatpants I had stashed away in the "house clothes" box, some socks, a pink Florida State University sweatshirt and two blankets. I didn't have any candles, no battery-operated radio, not even a flashlight. I curled up in bed, recounting the events of that evening, silently praying that things would change for me, and yet contemplating my next move.

94

Trickery

Chapter Fourteen

Four evenings with James came and went; sushi one night, Italian another, the other two nights we opted for our favorite seafood restaurants. By our sixth date, James wanted to create a more personal atmosphere for the two of us, so he invited me to dinner at his place. A man had never cooked for me before that night. I was more than anxious to experience a man of his caliber cooking for me.

The Fresh Market that James frequented was near my apartment, which was great since I didn't have a vehicle and no money for the bus let alone a taxi. When I wasn't dining with James, I was raiding whatever was left in the pantry, feasting on old canned goods and crackers that had kept well. I ate them sparingly, not knowing when I would be able to eat a full meal. I needed money, an occupation, and resources, but I received no responses and I wasn't hurting enough to beg for a minimum wage gig.

I dressed comfortably in an old, fitted pair of Seven Jeans and a cheap baby doll tee that read "Don't Be Jealous" on the front. He smiled as I walked to the SUV.

"What's funny?" I asked, getting into the vehicle.

"Nothing. You're gorgeous — even when you're not trying."
He continued to smile.

"What? Am I too dressed down? Is this okay?" I was fishing
for a compliment.

"No, no. You're fine. I have just never seen you dressed down
— which you look very nice, might I add." And there it was.
The groceries were already laid across the backseat, so our next
destination was his home.

The drive took almost 25 minutes, across the river and
through some wooded areas. The community had been hidden
behind towering spruce trees that lined the main road. James
signaled left then turned onto a gravel lot. For a moment, I could
see nothing there. The road meandered a bit, and seemed to have a
downward slope. As we descended, I could see a giant structure in
the distance. I didn't want to appear mesmerized by the size of his
house, so I pulled out my cell phone and began to thumb through
the near-empty phone book to busy myself.

"Oookay." He put the gear in park. "Would you mind
grabbing that bag from the floor? It has a bottle of wine in it, so
be careful."

96

Trickery

"No problem." I was trying not to admire my surroundings, as
if I were accustomed to such a lavish lifestyle.

A beautiful red brick design created the driveway, which
encircled the white fountain in front of his house. We took eight
steps up to the front doors, which was four times larger than the
average entryway. He placed a few bags on the ground to free
his hand in order to unlock the door. I playfully imagined that it
would come with keyless entry.

It smelled sweet inside, like scented candles had been burned
for hours. The marble floor of the foyer led to a book of stairs.
I followed him to the right, toward the kitchen — passing the
untouched living room and a dining room area with seating for at
least 16.

"You must have a large family," I said.

"Yeah, I do. Sometimes it's a good thing. Sometimes not so
good." We chuckled a bit.

"Do you do a lot of entertaining?" I staged questions to
distract him from my amazement, but I could tell he knew what I
was thinking.

"Well, when I'm not working, I typically have a few close
friends and some family over. But, for the most part, I go into the

city to see them. My place is really far and not too easy to find."
He placed the groceries on the counter then took the bag from me.
"You're welcome to browse around if you like."

"No. I'm fine. Maybe you can show me around later." He
smirked.

"I need to change. Would you like to stay in the kitchen? You
can sit at the counter if you want a front row seat." He started to
unbutton his shirt.

"Yeah, sure. That's fine."

He poured me a glass of wine then disappeared into a room
in the distance. After a moment I couldn't hear him or anything
at all.

The kitchen was spotless—not a dirty dish in sight, or a single
spatter on the counter or floors. There was a sink built into the
granite island counter in the center of the space —something I
had never seen before. There was no décor, only stainless steel
appliances and top of the line pots and pans hanging above the
island.

I sat in silence until I heard him coming up behind me.
He flipped a switch on the wall and the color blue splashed on
everything white within the kitchen. I turned to the ceiling to
floor windows directly behind me and noticed a swimming pool
illuminated with blue lights and surrounded by various poolside
furnishings.

"That's beautiful." I had to say it. His home deserved a
compliment.

"Thanks. It's one of the things I like most about this house,"
he said.

Never mind the huge rooms, expensive furnishings, or the
idea that maybe only 10 percent of Americans could afford to
live the way he was — it was the blue light shimmering from the
depths of his pool that was most amusing to him. I was certain to
believe that.

He lowered a few pots and pans, made some hot, sudsy
dishwater then cleaned them in the sink.

"I rarely cook now. So these things probably sat up there
collecting dust," he said with his back towards me.

"Did your ex-wife live here with you?" slipped out. He was
quiet for a moment.

"Yeah, she did. But let's not ruin our evening talking about
her. It's going pretty good so far." He placed a pot and a pan on

the stove and turned it on.

I didn't want to say all the wrong things, so I changed the subject by asking him about work. Afterwards we discussed the failing, improperly funded education system yet again, college Greeks and real estate. I was able to contribute on every subject.

The air began to fill with the aroma of fresh seafood and garlic being sautéed on the stove. Occasionally, he would stop and take a sip of wine while the food sizzled in the background. He made cooking seem so tireless and simple.

"We've known each other for a little while now." He stood in front of me on the other side of the bar. "Can I ask you something?" He took a sip.

"You could ask me anything, but if I'd answer is another question," I said jokingly to not upset him, but I was serious. When people begin a question with a question it is never a good thing. It's most likely something personal that they already know you would have a difficult time discussing.

"That day – the night that you came into the hospital – how did you get there?"

"An ambulance. You know that." I was sarcastic.

"You know what I mean." He was serious.

Trickery

I took a moment to think by taking a few small sips of wine. I knew that if I didn't respond it would affect the rest of the evening, and perhaps the relationship we were trying to establish. I was just upset that I hadn't come up with something ahead of time. In all honesty, I had tried my hardest to forget that the entire thing ever happened. My only reminder was the dark, empty apartment that I had gone home to every night.

"I was at a party with a friend — a really close friend. And everything got out of hand. There was an altercation between me and some guy and the next thing I remember I woke up in the hospital — and saw you," partially true. I stared directly into his eyes. It seemed as if he were trying to read me.

"Do you remember what the altercation was about?" He asked, turning away to check on the food.

I couldn't mention the word money at any point in the discussion. "Touching me," I said. That was also somewhat the truth.

"Well, where was your friend?"

"She left me there."

"I guess I can assume that you two are no longer friends." He turned to me again.

"No. I haven't seen her since that night."

"Do you know if she's okay? Something could have happened to her, too." Lines began to form in his forehead.

For a moment I thought of San — her safety. What if they had taken her and had done the same thing to her, or even worse, what if she was dead somewhere? What if they turned on her after she turned on me, then robbed us of all of our things in the apartment? What if they get away with it? I hadn't thought about it until then.

"Taj?" He walked over and placed his hand on mine.

I snapped out of it. "Yeah, I'm sorry."

"You okay?"

"I'm fine. Just thinking."

"I'm not going to get into your business," he leaned in closer, "but if that's what really happened that night, you would've told me then. And police involvement wouldn't have been such an issue."

"There is nothing more to it." I stuck to my story.

He backed away. "You ready to eat?"

I had lost my appetite but I wouldn't disappoint him by saying so.

As we ate, James insisted that we play the question game. Something that he'd made up in order to get to know someone as fast as possible. We were to answer each other's questions truthfully regardless of how embarrassing or personal it was. Through my participation in the game, I'd learned that he was the only son of five siblings, his father died of cancer when he was 11, and that he was the only person in his family to attend college. We also discussed keeping our intimate circle of friends as small as possible and trust, amongst other things. His past relationship with his ex-wife was a touchy subject, so I didn't mention it.

The question game was followed by a make-out session in his family room. The comfortable L-shaped leather couch was the focus of the room, while the 52-inch plasma, flat screen television provided a bit of entertainment when we came up for air. He was a great kisser, not giving too much tongue or too little. He knew when to break the lip-locking action and simply press his lips against mine. He did everything subtly. He didn't lean in and grab my waist. He didn't move his hand forward to touch and caress my breast. He didn't lay his hand on my thigh. He did nothing, as

99

Trickery

if the kiss was sufficient. I was baffled, questioning whether or not he desired to be with me. It made me want him more.

Positioned on the right side of him, I reached for his left hand that rested on his thigh. I interlocked my small fingers with his and tightened my grip while pressing my lips harder against his. I pulled him toward me. He gave in for a moment.

"Hold on." He leaned back for a moment. I was seriously waiting for him to tell me that he was gay and that he just wanted to be friends.

"Yeah? What's wrong?" I asked, wiping away lip gloss smeared on my chin and above my lip.

"Is this something that you want? I mean, I didn't bring you here to do this."

"I just want to be with you. Is it something that you want?"

"Never mind me. I wouldn't ever make you do something you don't want to do."

Then it all clicked. James saw me as the victim that had gone into the hospital three months prior to that moment. He didn't know how to approach me with the idea of having sex fully-knowing about the ordeal. I played into it.

100

Trickery

"I know. And I trust you." It sounded good at that moment. I slightly touched his chin and leaned in for a kiss.

He put his arm around me and pressed his palm against the small of my back, forcing me to lean back toward the arm of the couch. I allowed him to take control, and within seconds he was completely on top of me and we were interlocked in a kiss. He paused for a second and grabbed the remote. I assumed he would turn the television off, but he put changed the station to the 24 hour R&B Soul station. An oldie, Carl Thomas' "Summer Rain", was playing. After he placed the remote on the coffee table, he quickly lifted his shirt over his head. It was quite obvious that he worked out. By the impeccable cuts and bulges, I found myself wondering when he found time to create such perfection.

He became the aggressor, everything I wanted him to be. I could feel him growing through the basketball shorts he had changed into. I was pleased, so I decided to help him a bit by removing a piece of my own clothing, my jeans. It was quite a rushed move, but I didn't see a point in taking our time.

I could feel my wetness as he'd grind against me. We stayed locked in a kiss no matter what our lower halves were doing. I felt him maneuver his body, moving his hands to our lower region. He began to pull off his shorts with his hand, then inched them down to his ankle and completely off with his feet. There was warmth – breathtaking warmth that creates a rush of hormones straight to the brain and nearly causes an anxiety attack.

He also reached for my panties, but had no intentions of taking them off. He merely pulled them aside, then quickly attempted to insert himself.

"Wait." I pressed against his chest.

"What babe? What's wrong?" He was out of breath and as anxious as I was.

"Gotta condom?"

"No, I don't," he said remorsefully. "Do you want to stop? I know this is awkward. I just want you so bad right now." He kissed me again and I became lost in it. A minute went by as we kissed and I pretended not to notice that he was making a second attempt to penetrate me. I felt him inch it in. I moaned to signal my approval — my satisfaction. I realized how much I actually trusted James. At that moment, I trusted him with my life.

Trickery

Chapter Fifteen

No matter how many evenings I spent with James at his home, I never slept there. I was cautious not to overstay my welcome. I wanted to give him time to miss me, time to have the desire to come for me at the end of a long workday. I must admit that having him pick me up and drop me off at all hours of the night made me feel a bit remorseful, having him find out that I didn't have anything better to do than to sleep in his bed all day would have made me feel worse.

It had been three weeks since our first sexual encounter, and between his schedule and the busy schedule I pretended to have, we managed to have sex on eight different occasions. That particular night was no different.

James prepped the shower for us to freshen up from sweat and the exchange of other bodily fluids. We dressed and made our way out to the car. We held hands the entire ride back to my place and laughed about some of the highlights in the old Eddie Murphy "Raw" performance that we had rented from the classic section at Blockbuster.

I crossed my fingers in my mind, hoping that the management at the complex hadn't placed a bright orange eviction notice on my door. At that point, rent was almost 45 days past due and counting. As we pulled into the lot, I didn't notice any signage near the door. Coast is clear, I thought.

"Babe, would you mind if I use your restroom. I have to go."

I had never invited him into my apartment, and for good reason. I always came up with some excuse as to why he couldn't come in. I probably came across as being a slob having lied to him several times about it being too messy for me to have company over. I didn't want to recommend that he drive up to the local Gate gas station six minutes away in order to use a public restroom when one was only 20 feet away and available.

"Umm, sure. If you have to go." I was hoping he would say there was no urgency.

"Okay. Thanks."

He locked the doors and proceeded to the apartment, trying to make small talk along the way. I was quickly trying to cook up an excuse as to why I had no power. No genius idea would come to me than to pretend to not have a clue that they were off, so I went with that.

"Here we go," I said, pushing the door open.

"Damn, it's colder in there than it is outside," he said after a burst of cold air blew against our faces from inside the apartment.

"Yeah, I think I turned the heater off," I lied. I took a few more steps in and waited until he was inside before I attempted to flip on a light. I closed the door and went for the switch. Nothing happened. "Hmm, the bulb must have blown." He stood with his arms folded in the moonlight shining through the window. "Let me try another one."

"Where is your furniture? It's empty." He didn't seem concerned that we were standing in near-darkness.

"Umm – I sold it to make room for something I ordered at that new store – you know, the one in the town center." I flipped another switch, and I knew it was time for the real act to begin. "Oh wow."

"What?" I heard coming from a shadow.

"Something's wrong with the power." I walked to several light switches and flicked them on and off.

"Well, the people next door have power. I could see their lights when we walked up."

"That's strange. I'll look into it tomorrow and get it all

straightened out. I'll be fine for the night. The bathroom is this way." I grabbed his hand and rushed him to the bathroom inside the master bedroom where I knew the most moonlight would shine if I left the door open. Even in the dark I could tell that he was being extra-observant by his slow pace and lack of conversation.

"Just leave the door open and you can use the light shining through this window. I'm stepping out."

I sat on the edge of the bed in the corner of the room waiting to hear the last drip of urine splash against the toilet water. I heard him zip, flush, then run his hands under the faucet – cold I suppose.

"Tell me this—why have you been living in the dark? Is there something going on because I don't understand this?" He stood in front of me, arms folded again.

"What do you mean? I had power this afternoon. It was probably disconnected by mistake or something."

"You might want to keep your day job because lying is not your forte." He turned and walked back to the bathroom. "So you mean to tell me that a woman with power typically has three candles on her bathroom sink, two very visible flashlights, several D batteries strewn across the floor, and a load of blankets on her bed? I think the question is: how long have you been without power?"

105

Trickery

I didn't want to speak. I was embarrassed and ashamed. Crawling under a rock wouldn't have been enough. I would have rather been bludgeoned with one.

"Actually, for now, it doesn't matter," he continued, "get your things and let's go." He waited in the empty living room. I moved slowly in the bedroom, gathering some toiletries, underwear, and my favorite sweatshirt. Everything was in the laundry, which I had no money to wash.

We didn't speak the entire ride back to his house. I felt like a teenager after being chastised by her father for breaking curfew or sneaking out of the house or having sex while the parents were at work, but for some reason, I liked it. To know that he wanted what was best for me, to the point that he was upset when I didn't have it, made me realize how much he cared.

"We both need to get some rest. I have to be at the hospital by six." He opened the front door and I entered in silence.

We made our way to the bedroom and I undressed down to my panties and bra then climbed into bed next to him. He turned over and put his arm around my waist, kissed me on my neck, then told me goodnight. A sense of relief had come over me and it wasn't long before I shut my eyes completely, and went off to sleep.

The next morning he was gone. The place was quiet. There was a note on the nightstand, written on a paper towel from the bathroom, plain, unlike the floral printed paper towels in the kitchen. It read: Don't Leave.

Hungry, I threw on one of his T-shirts and went downstairs to raid the pantry for whatever I could find. I started at the fridge, which had been stocked with fresh fruits, some condiments, sandwich meat, bottled water and two percent milk. There was some toasted oats cereal in the pantry, so I poured a bowl, chopped up a banana and added milk.

The idea that I should go snooping around crossed my mind after breakfast, but the urge wasn't strong enough for me to actually do it. I just wanted rest, to lie down through the morning and possibly do absolutely nothing all day.

When James returned home that evening, I was sitting out by the pool. I had prepared a turkey club sandwich with items I found in the fridge and laid it on the counter. I left the kitchen light on, so I was able to see his smile from the pool before he looked in my direction and saw me sitting there. He picked up the plate, grabbed a bottle of water from the fridge and came out to join me.

"What a kind gesture." He sat down next to me, near the edge of the pool.

"It was all that I could do considering that you don't have too much to work with."

"I try not to keep food that I don't eat regularly. It goes bad too quickly. So, do you cook?"

"I'm pretty good in the kitchen. I like learning to make new dishes more than anything."

"Well, when I'm finished with this, we'll go to the store to get a few things."

"No problem."

James didn't bother to talk about the night before, or to ask me how long I was going to be staying around, or to ask about the occupation I proclaimed to have. Between bites of his sandwich, he talked about work — how a little girl had broken her arm by

Trickery

supposedly falling from a swing. He said he suspected child abuse because the parent's wouldn't allow the girl to speak when he questioned her about the incident. I found the story interesting.

We went shopping that evening, and I purchased some fresh vegetables, some poultry, a few steaks, and a few slices of tiramisu. That evening was similar to all the others I had spent there, except in reverse. Instead of sex and then a shower, we showered first, then had sex and fell asleep — together.

The following morning when I awoke, James wasn't there, but there was another note hidden slightly under a set of keys that read: Don't go far. I want to see you when I get home. Enjoy your day.

I walked through the kitchen to the garage, passing a piece of platinum colored plastic on the counter. It was the card he had used to purchase groceries. There was no note regarding the credit card, but I picked it up from the counter anyway. I opened the garage door and felt around in the dark for a light switch. Once I found it, I noticed a car more beautiful than I had ever rented in the past – a black Mercedes SL600. I initially stood in the doorway admiring the expensive piece of steel thinking of the many places that I could go, but wouldn't.

Trickery

The wood grain dash was clean, clear of even a speck of dust. The leather seats were warm and comfortable. It had been months since I sat behind the wheel of European-engineered steel. It had been too long. There was only 2500 miles on the car. "Damn — a nice ass car that he never drives. He's crazy as hell!" I said aloud and laughed to myself.

By 4:30 p.m. it was time to prepare dinner. The oven was set on broil and I placed a skillet on the stove to sauté some potatoes. The aroma of fresh herbs and broiled steak began to fill the air. Singing and humming songs that resonated in my mind from watching music videos, I floated around the kitchen. Last, I put a few ears of corn in boiling water, preparing to wrap them in foil with some butter and fresh herbs.

Ten minutes before James was due to arrive, I ran to the shower to freshen up and have the clean scent of Caress on my skin. Afterwards, I fingered my hair a little to separate the curls, and added a moisturizer to a few areas of my body that could use some extra softening — the elbows, knees and ankles. Then, I noticed something move in the corner.

"Oh my God!" I grabbed my chest, still wrapped in a towel.

James was in the room watching me. "Oh my God! You scared the hell out of me. How long you been standing there?"

He laughed. "You were just so sexy and I didn't want to disturb you." He loosened his tie, removed it, and then threw it on the bed. "How was your day?" He kissed me.

"Good. Dinner is ready whenever you are."

"I know. It looks appetizing too," he said, looking my body over. He loosened my towel, and as it fell onto the bed, I sat there, legs crossed and naked. He kissed my neck gently while he caressed my breasts. At that point, I knew it would be a while before we would go downstairs for dinner.

And it was. Dinner was cold after an hour of love-making. I turned on the oven and the stovetop to reheat the dishes. James poured two glasses of wine and sat at the bar watching me prepare his dinner, and grinning for some unknown reason.

"Wow." He laughed a little.

"What?" I turned around with a spatula full of sautéed potatoes.

"The only woman that has ever cooked for me was my mom. Oh, and maybe my oldest sister. You're something else. Beautiful and can cook — amongst one other thing." I smiled at him.

I wanted to ask what the hell his ex-wife was good for, but I figured it wasn't a good time to mention her. I couldn't think of any good time to mention her. He hadn't talked about her since our first date and he said just enough to let me know that their relationship existed but that he was completely over it. By the way he acted I couldn't tell that there wasn't any love there for her. I pictured her as some dainty housewife who was only good for spending his money, and possibly the reason they didn't work out.

"Do you dance?" he asked, breaking my train of thought.

"Like a stripper, a clubber or an artist?"

"None of the above," he chuckled, "just for fun — with a partner and not some random guy you meet and grind your ass on."

"I've never done it."

"Why don't we go out tonight? There is this spot with a live jazz band downtown — right on the riverfront. I know the owner. You interested?"

The invitation was shocking. James usually spent one night a week with the boys, if his schedule permitted of course. I

Trickery

learned a lot about Marcus and Tyson through conversations with James. Marcus had attended college with James, and Tyson was a colleague at the hospital. Both of them were married.

"Yeah, it sounds nice.""Well, get dressed after dinner and I'll take you."

"Do I have to dress up? I don't have anything nice over here to wear. My things are back at the apartment?"

"What apartment?" he asked sarcastically. "Then where did you go today?"

"Nowhere — I mean, I went around the block. That's all."

"Around the block where? You didn't go and get some things?"

"I didn't know I was supposed to go to my apartment. You didn't say that in your note."

"No. I left you my credit card. I figured you would go to the mall or town center or something to pick up a few things."

"I didn't know that's what you meant." I put a dish in front of him and laid a napkin topped with silverware next to it.

"Well, we'll chill out tonight, but you know what's on your agenda for tomorrow." He picked up his steak knife and pointed towards me as he spoke, "and don't go back to that apartment. There is no point."

Trickery

Before he could finish chewing his first bite, he was already cutting the tender, succulent meat for a second taste, an indication that I had done well.

Although James opened his home to me faster than anyone had, I still found it difficult to open up completely to him. Comfort stood in for love. He found it necessary to take care of me, and I found myself in need of him. I became a homebody. Everything I wanted was within those walls, but from time to time, while James was working, I would go into the town center to visit the spa or to do some shopping, but nothing else would interest me unless it was done with James: dinner, dances, movies, and so on.

I prepared dinner on nights that he didn't plan to take me out. We had great sex that took place in numerous locations within the house, outside the house, and even in some public places. Between our wild escapades and fancy dinners, there was no room for arguments.

Chapter Sixteen

Trickery

There was one other woman in James' life besides his mother and sister, which I had been waiting to meet for some time. Her name was Melinda, and she and James had been friends since childhood. There were several nights that he would come in from work, already engaged in conversation with her from his ride home. He would speak loudly when I was in the room, perhaps so that I wouldn't feel insecure about him conversing with another woman.

He described Melinda as the needy type, and although beautiful, would quickly turn a man away with her clinginess and urgency to wed — the typical woman to me. James had made arrangements for the three of us to meet up for lunch so that we could meet formally. Melinda suggested that we meet at a bistro downtown near the river and we both agreed.

It was windier than it typically was in the city. The breeze from the river sent chills up my blue satin skirt straight to my white lace panties beneath it. Walking toward the bistro, I considered that the fragrance from my freshly washed hair hypnotized those walking behind me along the sidewalk.

"Hey, James!" someone yelled in the distance. He stopped

and turned but couldn't pinpoint the source. "Over here, James."

There was a woman waving. She was petite — smaller than I was, less curvy. She wore a little black dress that kept very little to the imagination. Whatever breasts she did have were almost revealed completely. She only left about four inches of thigh to the imagination. Her smile was flawless but I wondered who would actually pay it any attention. James grabbed my hand and proceeded to introduce us.

"Hey Melinda!" He smiled big and leaned in to hug her. "This is Taj — my girlfriend."

"Hey. It's nice to meet you." I said shyly and reached out to shake her hand.

"Oh girl, give me a hug. It's so nice to finally meet you." We embraced shortly. "So do you guys want to dine on the patio or go inside?"

"Well, aren't you a bit cold?" I said from nowhere. "I mean, it's really chilly outside."

"Don't worry about me. I'm fine, but if you would like to go inside it's cool."

112

Trickery

The three of us walked in and were seated immediately. Melinda took her position at James' left, directly across from me. I tried to find objects to distract me from looking at her, but I was curious and wanted to examine every inch of the woman my man talked to regularly.

She had a small beauty mark on the right side of her face below her lip and when she smiled, she had one extremely deep dimple in her left cheek and a minor one on the right. Her eyes were naturally hazel, which went well with her hair that had been dyed a sunset auburn color and flowed beautifully past her shoulders.

"So, what do you two have planned for today?" She looked at me, obviously examining me as well, as she placed the napkin on her lap.

"Maybe some window shopping. I don't know." I looked at James. "Babe, what do you want to do?"

"Nothing in particular," he responded.

"Oh come on. It's one of your only days off. I know there is something that you want to do." She was moving in too closely. What he did on his days off was none of her concern.

"Oh believe me, we'll come up with something." I smiled.

We ordered a few appetizers and ice teas and for a moment discussed the poor quality of water in the St. John's River.

"I forgot to ask you — how is the family?"

"My mom is great. She and my sisters are in Houston looking after my grandmother who isn't doing so well. They should be back in a few weeks though. They're bringing my grandmother here." A few details he had yet to tell me.

"Wow! I'm sorry to hear that." She rubbed his hand as it rested on the table.

I cleared my throat. "Baby, what are we ordering as an entrée?"

"I don't know," he brushed me off, mind obviously in some other place. "My grandmother has lived a very long, fulfilling life, but none of us are ready for her to go yet."

"I can understand that. Whatever happens, you'll be able to handle it. How are your sisters taking it — and your nieces?"

"Okay! You guys ready to order?" the waitress interrupts to take our order.

"Melinda, what do you recommend?" He flipped through the menu.

"For you? I know how you are about what you eat and being physically fit and all, so I recommend the salmon. It's really good here — and really good for the body. Doesn't look like you need help in that area though." They both chuckled.

Trickery

"Excuse me?" I blurted out, frustrated and angered that she would bluntly make a pass at James in front of me.

"Babe, Melinda means nothing by it. We've been friends for so long and —"

"I didn't mean to be disrespectful. I apologize, Taj." I gave her the evil eye and maintained my composure for James' sake. I began to wonder if they had been more than friends, or if they were curious to know what being "more than friends" was like.

The waitress witnessed the whole ordeal. As an indication that she sided with me, she pleasantly asked to take my order first. Then she proceeded to James and Melinda with a hint of attitude.

"Can we just change the subject?" James asked.

"Sure." I agreed.

"We're having a big cookout for my grandmother and my nephew, Tyler, when he returns from Iraq in a few weeks. Will you be there, Melinda?"

"I'll have to check my schedule," she joked. "Sure, I'll be there."

"Taj, you'll get to meet the entire family then."

"Girl, his family is a trip. James becomes a certified mama's boy when he gets around them."

"Oh really?" I was curious.

"Yes. And uh oh, James, Taj is really pretty. You might have to watch her."

"What do you mean?" I asked.

"Oh, God. Let's not go there. My cousin is not a vulture." He stuffed his mouth with spinach and artichoke dip.

"I can't tell. She is more aggressive than most guys I know; she's just really smooth with it."

"Who is she talking about?" I asked James.

"My cousin, Seymone. She's a beautiful girl, but we're still wondering why the hell she's so into women. I mean — are no men out there good enough? I've tried to introduce her to several of my associates. She turned them down quick."

"Umm hmmm. I don't see how she could go without the strength and scent of a man. I can't.

"Are you sure about that, Melinda?" James asked, "ya know, you are still single. I figured you had crossed over on us."

Trickery

"Ha ha! You got jokes. I admire a beautiful lady when I see one, but that's always as far as it goes." She looked over at me. The drink specials menu in the center of the table distracted me. "What about you, Taj?"

"What?"

"Ever think about being with a woman?"

"Look, don't put my girl on the spot. She would never swing that way. I know her too well. I know exactly what she likes." He smirked.

"Ew! I've heard enough. Let's change the subject," Melinda said, taking a sip of her ice tea.

As they continued to converse, I thought of the secrets that I kept from James and how disappointed he would be if he found out about them. Although it occurred in the past, it could still effect the present and perhaps a future with him. Some men laugh at the idea of two women being committed to each other; others are disgusted by it. It's one thing to have been with other men, and another to have been with women. Secretly, most men develop insecurities. They'll work their ass off to be the best man we've ever been with, but no matter how hard they try, a man could never be the same as a woman.

Lunch ended abruptly when James declared to have a

headache. I rushed him home and away from Melinda quickly, with absolutely no hesitation. She seemed to be a nice person, but I couldn't help but wonder if she and James got along so well why they never made an attempt to be together. I was curious about that idea until one night, three days after our lunch date, when I overheard James talking from the other room — something he had never done before. I was in the middle of my dance aerobics video in the living room when he came in. He didn't use complete sentences and he spoke in a serious, forbidding voice.

"...whenever I'm ready...I'll do it on my time...not tonight... I understand."

I turned the television down a little so that I could hear him better.

"No, I don't want you to be with me when I tell her. You've done enough...thanks for understanding...soon...I'm excited too...the two of us."

I stopped the video and ran to the shower to keep from overreacting and so that James wouldn't see me crying. So many thoughts began to plague me at one time. For the first time since we had been together, I feared that I could possibly lose him. Instead of discussing it with him, I directed all of my emotions inward.

115

Trickery

Chapter Seventeen

Trickery

The drive to the restaurant was quiet. Frankie Beverly's greatest hits blared from the stereo system. Every once in a while he would tap the steering wheel with his right index finger to the beat. Whenever he looked over to me, I pretended not to notice. I felt like a lost puppy, one in foster care at the local shelter and was in dire need to be adopted. I was on my best behavior.

We arrived to a restaurant that he had never taken me to before. "Cypress" was lit across the front of the building. There was nothing fancy about it on the outside, no valet, no fancy entry way or revolving doors. The inside was small, everything white. There were only about twelve tables in the entire space, with a huge bar dividing the room into halves. Candles were lit on each table, and slow, melodic music could be heard coming from some place unknown. There was a hat and coat rack too close to the entry, which I couldn't entrust to hold the Burberry coat I had just purchased. The hostess was a very petite white girl, probably no older than 19 or 20, and perhaps working to make some money while in college. She had emerald eyes and blonde hair that was swept neatly into a ponytail. Her smile was reminiscent of pictures I had seen plastered on the walls of my dentist's office – beautiful.

She didn't greet us. She didn't ask, "How many?" She smirked a little, then walked us to a table in the corner of the restaurant.

"Do you know her or something?" I asked James, removing my coat and laying it across the unoccupied chair at the table.

"No babe. I don't." He sat down and slightly loosened his tie.

I chose not to order an appetizer and so did James. I assumed that he was hungry given a comment he'd made earlier. For our entrees, we feasted on a seafood boil of shrimp, fish, clams, mussels and scallops. James also ordered a fancy shrimp and grits dish. He made small talk about the restaurant, the chef's techniques, and possible future business ventures. I listened.

When the waitress offered to bring us some dessert, James replied to bring us "something special". I imagined a nice chunk of chocolate cake, or a velvety slice of New York style cheesecake. On her serving tray was simply a box – about a foot long and wide – wrapped in red paper with a black ribbon tied around it.

"What's this?" I smiled as she handed the package over to me.

"Well, you have to open in to find out," James responded. "That will be all ma'am," James excused the waitress.

"So, is this what you've been up to today? Awww. You thought of me. You're so sweet baby."

Impatiently, he said, "Yes, I know. Open it!"

"Okay. Okay." I placed the box on the table and slowly tugged at the ribbon. I expected a blue Tiffany box carrying some new jewels or perhaps keys to a new Lexus or something. As I lifted the lid from the box, I saw the color blue. Removing the lid further, I revealed metal and a rubber material. It was a stethoscope. I was puzzled and I knew he could tell by the expression on my face.

"Surprised?" he asked, leaning in to reach for it.

"Well, I really don't know what to make of it." I really didn't.

"Well, this is the stethoscope that was used when you came into the hospital almost a year ago. With this I monitored the rhythm of your heartbeat, I experienced what it was like for you to inhale and exhale — to feel your chest rise and sink so delicately with each breath. It became my mission to take care of you."

He pulled the tool from the box and placed them in my ears. "Now listen. Breathe slowly." He pressed the other end to my chest, "Can you hear that?"

Trickery

"A little. Yes."

He removed it from my chest then pressed it against his. "Can you hear this?"

I paused for a moment, waiting for silence. Once I found a break in the music and the wait staff chatting with each other in the corner, I noticed that his heart was pounding.

"It's faster than mine. Is that normal babe?" I was curious.

"It is when you're doing this." He pulled a small box from his coat pocket and kneeled on the floor next to my chair.

"Oh my God. Oh my God." I was nervous.

"Taj, I have been there for you since the very first day that we met. I have loved you and taken care of you in every way I know how. I live to know that you're safe, and not in need of anything or anyone. I know it hasn't been long, but baby I want forever with you. So can I be all that you need for the rest of your life?"

"Yes, baby. Yes!" A tear began to stream from somewhere. My chest tightened. He embraced me like he never had before then placed the platinum, three-carat, round cut, diamond ring on my finger. I turned to look at the hostess, smiling. She smiled back at me then went back to her place at the front of the restaurant.

Trickery

James later told me that Melinda had helped him pick out the ring, and that she'd wanted him to give it to me sooner, and even be present at the proposal. At that moment, the phone call in the other room all made sense. I felt so ashamed, but I held on to this happiness and decided it was better not to confront him about the incident.

Chapter Eighteen

James had told his family of the engagement via telephone conversation three days before they arrived home from Houston. I had yet to meet them, and I wasn't as excited as I was prior to the proposal.

At the cookout, everyone seemed preoccupied with cooking, serving food, supervising the children. There were no formal introductions. I sat in the living room area alone and observed while James talked to various relatives. My skirt began to rise as my legs shook rhythmically, a nervous gesture from childhood. Staring through the kitchen, beyond the group of men gathered around the table, in line for a second helping, my eyes wandered for him. Anything was better than catching the eye of one of James' sisters or his mother.

"So, what's this I hear about a new house?" Janice, James' sister, asked as she entered the room and took a seat.

I was distracted by all of James' childhood photos on the wall. There was even a picture of him and a man I assumed was his father. James appeared to be about 9 years old; both of them were shirtless, flexing their muscles for the camera.

"A new house! I ain't heard nothing about ya'll moving," his mother butts in.

I parted my lips to reply when James walked into the living room, holding a frosted glass of red wine. His presence grabbed our attention as I stared in wait of a response from him – to have the spotlight taken from me.

"Well?" Janice stared harder, threatening me to answer.

"There isn't a new house mother. That's why you haven't heard." He made his way over to me and sat slowly, placing his hand gently on my thigh for balance. "We're just having some construction on a few areas of the house, just to make some of the spaces larger."

"Hell, you already have plenty room. What she need all them rooms for? She don't got no kids," Janice spoke as she reached over and shoved a mouthful of homemade mashed potatoes into her toddler's mouth. "And I don't see the two of you ever —" she started, but was distracted by the toddler's behavior as he threw the mashed potato-saliva combo unto her blouse.

I nudged his arm and he looked at me, capturing the frustration embedded on my forehead. I squeezed tighter, unable to wrap my hand around his bicep. His body was something magical, maintained by his twice-a-day workouts — in the morning before work and in our bedroom at night. His light brown sugar complexion seemed topped with the smoothness of honey. There was a silent "ding!" when he smiled, like in cartoons. Even after a year, my chest would still sink into my stomach at his touch.

"And when was the last time you been to see your daddy?" his mother asked with an attitude, as though I had made him forget about his deceased father.

"Last Tuesday, Ma. You know I put flowers on Daddy's grave once a month."

"Mm. Hm. You take lil' missy here with you."

"Yes, ma'am. I've gone to his gravesite," I responded politely. "I think it's time," I whispered to James.

"But we've only been here a half hour. Why don't we go into the dining room for a while," he lifted the hair from my face and tucked it behind my ears. "Then we can go if you like."

He took my hand and led me to the most crowded space in the house. His mother's home was large enough to house at least 15 comfortably, and more than 80 in social settings, yet another product of James' success. The ceiling-to-floor dining room windows revealed the well-lit pond beside the house as well as the guest house. The space was a true masterpiece, reduced by tasteless ceramic artifacts and artificial flower arrangements bought from the local flea market, reminders of where they'd been. There are six bedrooms, none fully decorated. There were bunk beds in three of them, intending to maximize the space. Many of the walls were ruined by the dirty hands of infants after play or a meal, needing a good scrubbing.

"Okay people, let's make a toast." James led by pouring a glass of champagne; many filled their glass to the brim. He handed it over to me, winked an eye, and smiled as he focused his attention to the crowd.

"I have to say we are blessed. Tyler is back home from war, and in one piece. I thank you," he said, directing his speech to his cousin, "for your dedication and sacrifice, for your family, and for your country. 'Cause believe me, no one else would have done it." The crowd laughed at his remark. "So for that, and to welcome you back home, there is a brand new Lexus parked in the front yard just for you."

I gasped. It was unexpected and had not been discussed with me first. The family rushed the "cheers" then scattered outside to get a look at Tyler's new ride. It was not the time to be confrontational with James. I hid my anger with a half-ass smile that helped me keep my cool. Janice stared directly at me as she drank the glass of champagne in one gulp, awaiting my breakdown.

Trickery

"Oh wow James! A new Lexus! Um, that sure is a pretty car out there. Don't you think Taj?" She teased.

"Yeah, it's — it's very nice." I took a sip of champagne and attempted to dismiss myself from the room. James grabbed me and placed an arm around my shoulder, knowing that I wouldn't make a scene by breaking away from him.

"Tyler, why don't you take your Aunt Taj here outside with you so that she can get a better look at the car? It was her idea, you know."

"Really? Aunt Taj? You really have good taste," his 5-foot-6 figure stood in James' shadow as he reached out to take my hand.

"Oh, okay yeah. Let's take a look. I didn't get to see what he actually brought from the dealership. I hope you like it though. You deserve it." I lied. There is nothing more special about this kid than any others who went over to serve our country besides the fact that he had a successful doctor for an uncle who was willing to please others through his checkbook.

The party died down after everyone had a glimpse of the brand new, fully loaded white Lexus parked in the driveway. Several cousins piled in to take photos behind the wheel as if it were their car, which would probably show up on Myspace or some other site where fools can look like ballers and unattractive women claim photos of models or movie stars as their own.

I overheard James' cousin sharing some of the family business with a first-time visitor as I was standing on the front porch.

"Yeah, that's my cuz. He a rich man, you know."

"What he do?" A young girl, perhaps his date for the evening, inquired.

"Well, he's a doctor now, but man, if you would have known him 10 years ago – "

"What was up with him then?" she asked, but I was curious to know myself.

"He was a screw up! His daddy died and left my aunt in the poorhouse. James didn't make it any better. He gave his mom a hard time. It wasn't until he met his ex-wife that someone was able to talk some common sense into him. That was all she was good for though." He laughed it off. "He always feels like he owes people something. He'll learn that he can't help everybody."

Trickery

I stood in the shadows, hoping that I could learn more, but the two of them walked farther into the front yard.

Keys rattled behind me as Seymone made her way to the front door. She reached out to give me a hug, "It sure is good meeting you, Taj."

Seymone reminded me a lot of myself, young, soft-spoken, classy and even a bit mysterious. She had a pair of the longest legs I'd ever seen, a complexion that screamed milk chocolate perfection and eyes like water, not being able to discern their true color. Her hair was short, which added a hint of sophistication to the package.

"Okay sweetheart. It's really nice finally meeting all of you." I hugged her, and got a whiff of her perfume. I melted for a moment. "What are you wearing? You smell so good."

She whispered, "It's a secret. I might tell you later. I just might." She gave a sexy grin and walked out of the room. My eyes followed her feet, admiring the 3-inch BCBG stiletto pumps that I swear I'd seen in a magazine somewhere.

"Are you leaving, Seymone?" I called after her.

"No. I'm just stepping outside for a cigarette. I'll be back in a moment."

I returned to the living room and buried my face in my hands. It was one of the most uncomfortable positions I had ever been in, and James didn't help to make it any better. It wasn't the idea that he had spent so much money on a vehicle that was intended for me, but that he hadn't even talked to me about it. I was in the dark with a lot his decisions and interactions with other people. I was a separate entity and couldn't mesh with any of his other dealings, and I accepted that position on many levels. My only wish was that he would have selected a better day and time to leave me out of the loop.

The front door slammed shut then I heard two women giggling. I could make out the clangor of Seymone's gold bangles, but the other woman's voice sounded familiar as well. They spoke as they walked into the dining room area, but I would briefly lose sight of them as they disappeared behind the three pillars that separated the large foyer from the living room.

The other woman was an inch or two shorter than me, a little lighter, and wore a blue strapless corset dress that hugged her body in all the right places, but I couldn't see her face. I wondered where James was — if he knew this person. Curious, I stood up slowly from my seat, grabbed my glass of champagne from the end table, and walked in the direction the two women had gone.

Trickery

After a few steps I came across them, standing around the dining room table. I stood in the doorway for a moment; both of their backs were toward me. I examined the mystery woman's body from my position and her interaction with Seymone. There was some familiarity in her movements and in the sound of her voice, but nothing more familiar than the tattoo on her left shoulder.

"Taj. Hey, I want you to meet my friend," Seymone said, pulling at the woman's arm to turn and greet me. She hesitated, then turned slowly.

"Hello, Taj. It's nice to meet you." She smiled.

It was her — the ghost from my past. She hadn't changed a bit. She was still as beautiful as I remembered her, but the thought of how beautiful she was became overshadowed by my memory of what occurred the last time I saw her. And she was smiling at me.

"Likewise," I said, taking a sip of champagne while looking directly at her. I couldn't make a scene. No one was supposed to know about her. I wondered how much Seymone had revealed about me to her — if San knew about my engagement. I wondered if she would jeopardize it — if she was there to hurt me again.

"Taj, I wanted to invite you to a track meet for the kids that I coach at the high school. San won't be able to make it, so I would like for you to come if you're not busy."

San's eyes wandered around the room, trying her best to remove herself from the conversation. It was apparent that they were lovers — primarily by how close they stood to each other, how they touched, and how they smirked at each other. I was taken back for a moment, to what it was like being with a woman, but the thought was short-lived. James walked into the room.

"There you are, Taj. I was wondering if you were ready to wrap it up here and go home." He stood behind me and wrapped his arm around my waist.

"Oh, and San, this is my cousin, James." She smiled at him and nodded her head. "James, I was just inviting Taj to the track meet tomorrow. I know you'll be working, but it's the last meet of the year and I would really like to see some of my people in the stands."

Trickery

"Taj, you should go. Will you be going?" he asked San.

"Oh no, I have a meeting. We'll probably do lunch afterwards or something," she responded.

"Well, Taj, you should be able to make it, right?" Seymone asked again.

"Sure. I'll be there."

I was in a tight situation. I didn't want her to think that I didn't want to be supportive. She was a very close relative to my fiancé, and although San said that she wouldn't be there, I didn't want her to get the impression that it mattered, as truthful as it might have been.

I could barely sleep that night. I thought of San — ways to kill her and get away with it. I thought of my past life and secrets that I was afraid would be revealed to James. Regardless of the many thoughts that raced through my mind, my life had to continue with James. I refuse to say that he was the love of my life. Love had nothing to do with it. I can admit that he was my only answer to a life of normalcy, an escape from the edgy world of being a "showgirl," borderline prostitute, and a drug addict. But damn, I missed getting high.

Chapter Nineteen

I owned only two pairs of tennis shoes; one was an all-white pair of Adidas and the other was a European-style pair of Jordan's for women. My short denim shorts and blue halter paired wonderfully with my Jordan's, so I slid them on in preparation for the track meet. James was at work, as usual, so it was quiet in the house. His work schedule became more frustrating by the day and I rarely ever saw him. Besides that, there were no other particular thoughts circling my mind, just preparing myself for a day in the sun, maybe even a bit of cheering here and there.

Once I arrived at the school, I parked the Mercedes SL600 at the back of the lot, away from reckless teenage drivers. The lot appeared desolate. The onlookers were already in the stadium cheering on the runners. I was late, but far from rushing.

"Hey! Excuse me!" I heard a male voice yell from across the lot. He closed the trunk of his all-terrain blue Hummer H2 and was hurriedly trying to catch up with me. I stopped in my tracks and shielded my eyes from the sun as I tried to look off in the distance.

"Yeah?" I said, and flashed him a little smile.

He was about 6-foot-3, an even-toned dark chocolate

complexion with a well-lined goatee and a freshly shaved head. I could see the outline of his pectoral muscles bulging through his t-shirt. His forearms alone were fascinating.

"How you doing today?" he asked, slowing his stroll.

"Do I know you from somewhere?"

"Maybe." I caught a whiff of his cologne. Damn, he smelled nice.

I thought, this is probably one of my old clients.

"Nah cutie, we don't know each other." Whew!

"Then what's your name? I'm Taj." I reached out to shake his hand.

"Kelvin Ross." He shook my hand.

"Hmm — why does that name sound familiar?"

"Well it should. I'll tell you why later. So can I get your number?"

"Whoa, fast guy. I'm engaged." I flashed him a glimpse of the rock.

"Engaged isn't married. I'm sure your man wouldn't mind if you had friends. Let me take you out."

"Well, I don't know if I —"

He lifted his arm to check the time on his diamond-studded Rolex and I lost my train of thought. "Look, take my number. I'm running late for a meeting, but I want you to call me." He licked his lips.

"What is it?"

I pulled my phone from my pocket and stored the number. We gave each other a quick hug goodbye and he ran back to the truck and drove away. I continued on to the track where there had to be at least two hundred spectators. Then I paid 75 cents for a can of Coke and found a seat on the third row of the concrete bleachers between a heavy-set white woman and group of Hispanic teenage boys.

After a few minutes passed, I spotted Seymone on the far end of the field, talking to her athletes. A group of students were running the 400 meters while she assembled her group to run the relay. She was aggressive, not exactly what I expected from her. Her body language oozed confidence and authority – extremely attractive features.

Seymone looked in my direction, and held the position as if she was trying to make sure it was me. I stood up and waved as hard and as fast as I could. When she didn't respond to my signal,

Trickery

I sat down again. Then someone tapped me on the shoulder. I turned my head slightly.

"I don't think she saw you." It was San. She had come to the track meet after all. My chest sank into my stomach.

"What the hell?" I attempted to stand and she pressed my right shoulder to keep me from moving.

"Don't make a scene. Seymone could see you."

"I don't give a damn! Let me go!"

"I think you care more than you think you do. Come on future Mrs. Doctor Carter." She giggled.

I turned to look at her. There was something different about her, but it wasn't physical. Whoever the person was in front of me, I had never known her.

"So, how have you been?" she asked, bending over to tie her shoe.

"Making it. Come on. Let's cut out all the small talk. Why do you even think you can talk to me? I should kill you right now." The lady next to me looked at the both of us then pretended to follow the activities on the track.

"I know. And I don't blame you. There is a lot that I could say, but I can't say it here."

"I don't want to hear anything you have to say, San."

"But you will. I know you will. I'll be at the coffee house we used to go to tomorrow around three. I'll see you then." She stood up and walked away, grabbing a bag of peanuts from the girl at the bottom of the bleachers before she disappeared.

I was being blackmailed. Initially San's behavior seemed outlandish, but then I thought of Sarai, possibly for the first time in more than a year. It was evident that San was making me pay for the decisions that I had made that seemed so long ago. Seeing San again reminded me of the hurt I endured, both physically and mentally, and the consequence of letting people in. I wanted to run in the other direction, hide even. For my protection, I knew that walls had to be built.

Seymone never looked my way after all. San already confronted me, so I had no fear of seeing her again when I went to greet Seymone after the meet. She smiled big and thanked me for coming. It felt good being supportive of someone else, but if I'd known that she wouldn't even notice I was there until the end, I would have stayed at home.

The next morning I didn't awake until after ten. James and

I had been up all night watching various old school videos on YouTube because we both had difficulty sleeping. By sunrise, James was gone. I could never get used to his long work hours, or him being called away at all hours of the night, or not being there for holidays, even my birthday. If I had to analyze a side-by-side comparison of my life before James, when I was alone and performing shows, to life with him, I would say they were nearly identical. Material things were easy to come by, but no one was there.

I knew I had to meet up with San, primarily to keep her mouth shut, but a potential new friend sparked my curiosity. He was mysterious, yet so familiar. And I was eager to learn more.

I sent him a text that said, "Hey u. Busy?"

"Who is this?" he responded.

"Damn, u give ur number out like that?"

"I think I know who this is. R u 2 busy 4 me right now?"

"NOW?"

"Yeah. I'm leavin in 2 days for business. Meet me somewhere."

I closed my phone, thought for a moment, then replied.

Chapter Twenty

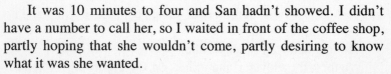

It was 10 minutes to four and San hadn't showed. I didn't have a number to call her, so I waited in front of the coffee shop, partly hoping that she wouldn't come, partly desiring to know what it was she wanted.

By 4:15 p.m. San pulled up next to me in a brand new black Escalade with black rims and dark tinted windows. She rolled down the window slightly, only revealing her bug-eyed frames and freshly glossed lips.

"Hey. Follow me." She put her vehicle in reverse and proceeded to back away before I had the opportunity to respond.

We drove for at least six minutes through neighborhoods in the historic side of Jacksonville that most of us know as Riverside or Avondale. The area is home to people we consider being "old money," having wealth that extended from generations. We passed Memorial Park, where my mom took me as a kid, across the street from the new Publix shopping center, and arrived at the newly built condos on the edge of the river.

We parked and I hesitated for a moment before I exited the car.

"What's this?" I asked, walking around to the back of the car to meet her.

"This is my place." She secured her Louis Vuitton bag on her shoulder.

"Why are we here, San? I thought you said to meet at the coffee shop."

She stopped walking and turned to me, "Yes, meet there." Then she continued walking.

I followed, wondering what surprises lie within the building. Although the sun was fairly high, the garage was extremely dark and quiet. A white brunette was unloading groceries from her Coca-Cola colored Lexus while holding a toddler in her arms. She struggled with the load and I considered asking if she wanted help, but the situation deterred me from making an offer.

San swiped a key card and we entered the building through a set of glass double doors. The lobby smelled of cinnamon and fresh baked chocolate chip cookies. San walked slowly toward the elevator and I followed not too far behind her.

"Good Afternoon!" the receptionist exclaimed, leaning forward in his seat to get a good look at us.

"Hey Manuel. How's it going?" San replied.

"Just wishing I was off and able to join you ladies today." His hair was curly – most definitely of some Hispanic origin – and he had very rigid teeth, sharp.

She laughed. "Not today, babe."

We took the elevator and exited on the eighth floor. "You'll have to excuse my place. I've been pretty busy lately."

When she opened the door, it revealed an amazing view of the St. John's River—no curtains, no blinds. Her place was furnished with contemporary pieces that I recognized from the West Helm showroom. Scattered around the space were 12 medium-size boxes. She walked over to one and opened it.

"This is why I brought you here," she said, removing the contents of the box.

"This is a very nice place, San," I said, staring down at the white, plush carpet.

"Thanks. I've come a very long way." She laid the paper packaging on the granite countertop that separated the living room area from the kitchen, reached into the box again and withdrew a paperback book. "I owe this to you."

I read the cover —"Operation: Survival" it read. The back cover revealed that it was a nonfiction account of a woman's life who had been abused as a child, victimized by her lovers, worked as a prostitute, and who had lost someone very close to her. Below the synopsis of the book was a picture of San, smiling.

She had written a book, had actually had someone print it, and was in the process of selling it. I wondered if I was in it — if she had used my real name. I wondered how long it had taken her, if it was the same piece she began when we were still together. I wondered if any of it was true.

I flipped through the pages, trying to take in as much of the information as I could digest before turning the page. The first page read: "An inch toward healing is better than none at all. My ruler, please." I was puzzled.

"No need to hurry. I'm giving that to you." I stopped flipping through the pages and looked at her. "Taj, if it weren't for you I wouldn't have had the courage to do this. And if it weren't for the experiences that you allowed me to share with you, I would have nothing extraordinary to talk about."

"So this book is about me?" I pressed the book to my chest.

"No, me. You are in some chapters, but not throughout." I looked puzzled. "I didn't include your real name. I call you T.J. in the book." I obviously appeared relieved because she returned a smile.

133

Trickery

"How long did it take you to complete?"

"A little over three months."

"And you're selling these?"

"Yeah. I published them myself, so I'm in the process of shipping them out to some local distributors and selling them on my website."

"Oh." I placed the book on the counter and took a seat on the barstool. San came behind me and gently touched my shoulder.

"Taj, I've wanted to talk to you for so long. I wanted to find you and make sure that you were okay." I looked away from her. "I know it may mean nothing now, but I was stupid. I was greedy. I was insecure. I —"

"Almost had me killed? Is that what you were going to say?" Her eyes began to water as her lips trembled. "What is there to cry for now? I was traded. For what? You betrayed me. You hated me so much that you didn't care to watch me die in that hotel room."

My head began to throb and my face and limbs became warm to the touch. The flood gates were opened. But I didn't wail because of hurt, but because of anger. I wanted to reach out and choke her, kick her in the stomach, slap her around until she lost consciousness. I didn't. Instead, I dried my eyes, regained composure, and stared at her seriously. "Are we done here?"

"Taj, I think we have a lot more to talk about. I'm not ready for you to leave yet."

"Do I look like a friend to you? It wasn't my choice to come here. So, if you've said everything you need to say, then I'm leaving."

"I didn't force you to come, Taj."

"Oh really?" I asked sarcastically.

"What?" She thought for a moment. "Do you think I'm blackmailing you or something?" She giggled.

"Well, things have been working out well for me. I don't want anything to jeopardize my current situation."

"He doesn't know, does he?" She cut me off.

"My relationship with him is none of your damn business, San."

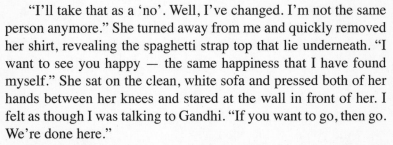

"I'll take that as a 'no'. Well, I've changed. I'm not the same person anymore." She turned away from me and quickly removed her shirt, revealing the spaghetti strap top that lie underneath. "I want to see you happy — the same happiness that I have found myself." She sat on the clean, white sofa and pressed both of her hands between her knees and stared at the wall in front of her. I felt as though I was talking to Gandhi. "If you want to go, then go. We're done here."

I could tell that there was much more that she wanted to say, or I at least wanted her to volunteer where the hell she pulled all this happiness from. She had obviously been exploring the self-help book section.

I picked up my keys from the counter and walked towards the door, not desiring to speak another word to her.

"And I would appreciate it if you didn't mention anything to Seymone," she said as I opened the front door.

"I see I'm not the only one with secrets." I turned to leave and closed the door behind me.

Trickery

Chapter Twenty-One

One particular weekend, four months into our affair, Kelvin and I planned to meet at the Sawgrass Marriott at Jacksonville Beach. James was working for the entire weekend – nothing out of the ordinary – so I made plans to spend time away from home, which at that point was also not out of the ordinary. James and I were engaged, but no plans had been made towards us actually exchanging vows. Our life at home had become routine, and we seemed comfortable with the way things were. It made me nervous. The presence of a void intensified, and because of that, I feared the worst. I couldn't be without, or be in that place again. I thirsted for more security. And oh, the places I found it.

Kelvin had reserved the room and convinced the staff to issue me a key until he arrived. I walked into the spacious two-bedroom villa, dropped my bag of toiletries in the closest bedroom, and made myself comfortable. The balcony overlooked the golf course, so I watched as white men teed off and jumped in their little carts to chase the balls. A man walking in to a room with a woman on the couch lazily watching television is possibly the least sexy sight, so I attempted to focus my attention on the activities occurring outside our hotel window.

I heard a click. The door unlocked and Kelvin appeared in the hallway, wearing a crisp polo shirt and jeans.

"I tried to call you," he said. "What's up with your phone?" He was a bit flustered, and had the appearance of a man who had just run up eight flights of steps.

"I don't know. I didn't hear it ring. Maybe it's just poor reception." I continued to watch the men on the golf course, pretending it didn't matter that he was in the room.

"Well, hello." He slowed his breathing, then put his arms around my waist and kissed me slowly.

"Hey. I missed you."

"Really? What'd you miss?"

"Everything." I smirked.

"Well show me." He stared at me for a moment. Then I took his hand and led him to the master bedroom.

Our night ended with our sweating bodies lying next to each other in soaked, white sheets. There was nothing else to be said. We slept peacefully through the night, and by morning he was gone again.

Checkout wasn't until noon, so I had time to shower and get myself together before I was due back home. I removed the clothes that I wore the day before from the closet, checked them for wrinkles, and then put them back on. There was no reason to put on a fresh face, so I pulled my hair back into a loose ponytail and threw on a pair of shades.

"I would like to check out, please." I said to the receptionist behind the counter.

"What's the name?" she started pecking on the keyboard.

"Ross." I said loudly.

"Okay, I have two guests with the last name Ross staying with us this weekend. May I have a first name or your room number, please." She was being polite, but was making me impatient.

"Kelvin Ross." I retorted.

"Taj?" I heard a female voice behind me.

I turned quickly. It was Melinda, dressed in business attire and carrying a briefcase.

"Oh, hi," I said nervously, wondering how long she had been behind me.

"A little far from home, aren't we?" she said sarcastically.

"No, not far at all." I know she wasn't expecting for me to explain myself to her.

136

Trickery

"Then I'm wondering what someone who's not far from their place of residence, who actually lives in a multi-million dollar home 20 minutes from here, is doing checking out of a hotel." She paused for a moment and noticed the disgust in my expression. "Oh, and get this, a hotel room that is registered under a man's name who is not her fiancé." She made it worse.

"I guess that's for me know, and for you to continue to wonder about." I grabbed the printout from the receptionist, who was listening to the whole ordeal, and walked away.

When I reached the corridor leading to the parking garage, Melinda was right behind me. Her hand pressed against my shoulder, signaling for me to stop a moment.

"What is it, Melinda?"

"Listen. I don't know you. I really don't give a damn about ever knowing you, but I do know James. I know that he has been hurt, deeper than most people can imagine."

"Don't you think I know my fiancé a little more than you?" I pushed her hand off of my shoulder.

She pressed her lips together for a moment. "Now he's your fiancé? So, just because you sleep with someone, that means you know them better? You're clueless."

137

Trickery

"So what? Should I expect for you and him to have a little chat about this or something?" What have I gotten myself into? I thought.

"No. I am not that kind of woman. As much as I hate to see my friend hurting, revealing your dirt to him myself wouldn't even do me justice."

"So, this is about you?" I asked.

"You're damn right. It won't be long before the things you've done in the dark come to light. And when they do, I'll be there to console him, but this time, I'm not letting him go."

"What do you mean this time?"

"Your days are numbered," she said as she turned to walk away.

I ran after her to continue our discussion, and possibly for her to guarantee that James wouldn't hear about the situation, an admission of guilt.

"So you mean this entire time, you and James have been involved? You're such a low down, dirty ho." I attempted to use reverse psychology.

"No, but if it makes you feel better while you're unpacking

your overnight bag and washing your dirty lingerie, then so be it."
It didn't work. I stood there for a moment, thinking of what to say
next. She placed her briefcase on the ground. "Look, we all have
secrets, but it is unfortunate when the people we love are hurt by
them."

"I don't need a lesson on life, Melinda. I know—"

"Does James talk about his ex-wife?" She cut me off. I shook
my head, curious about what she would say next. "I know. I bet
you don't even know her name. But what you should know is that
her secrets are the reason that they're not married today. Most
importantly, her secrets caused James to develop a few of his
own."

"What? What secrets?"

She picked up her briefcase. "He's your fiancé. Maybe you
should get to know him."

That was the second time she walked away from me while I
was attempting to talk to her. I refused to follow her around like
a puppy, so I walked out to the garage, got into my car, and drove
away. Melinda's words resonated in my mind for the entire drive
home. Secrets?

Trickery

Chapter Twenty-Two

"I hate the way you've been moping around here lately." James picked up his reading glasses from the kitchen table and proceeded to read the newspaper, still dressed in his Christmas-colored morning robe.

"I'm fine baby. Just had a lot on my mind." I was wrapped in a white blanket and lounging in the chair next to him, staring at the pool from the window.

"I hate to pry, but it's hard to understand what could be so wrong." He placed the newspaper down on the table. "Maybe we both could use some relief. Let's drive to Miami for the weekend." He became excited. "We can get a spot on South Beach and chill for a little while."

"No baby. That sounds great, but I'm really not in the mood for a vacation." I turned to look him. "I just need some time."

Looking in his direction, I caught a glimpse of the television. And for the first time, the two men with whom I was involved were in the same room. I couldn't hear, and I didn't want to appear overly interested in the figure on the television, so I sat there, eyes widened, and taking in every image of him. Kelvin was being interviewed wearing a Denver Broncos jersey while standing on a field, seemingly after a game. The station was playing the highlights of the previous night's game. His name flashed across the bottom of the screen, confirming my thoughts. I felt as though someone had put a bend in the hose of my air supply. Oh my God! He's an athlete. I could feel James' eyes studying my every movement, my composure. I had to snap out of it, and quickly.

We sat in silence for a moment. It became apparent that the both of us were thinking of what to say next.

"Get dressed," he whispered, looking above the frames of his glasses.

"For what?" I said, very distracted.

"Dress nice. Not too fancy though." He stood and walked out of the room.

My stomach was in knots, and I cringed a little more with each thought of Kelvin.

I went to the closet and I heard James messing around in one of the spare bedrooms. The black Chanel dress fit too snug, so I went with the navy blue Calvin Klein pant suit, slipped on a pair of Nine West pumps (probably the cheapest pair I owned) and the diamond studded watch James had bought me for Christmas.

Trickery

I was on the bed fastening my earrings when James appeared in the doorway, wearing an all black suit with a beautifully patterned tie with crimson diamond shapes throughout. He drew the tie closer to his neck, and looked at me for approval.

"I like it. You look nice baby," I said, looking him up and down.

"You're beautiful. But that's nothing new."

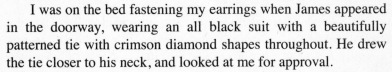

We were in the car for almost 20 minutes when James turned into a gravel lot off of the busy highway. The sign out front read: United Church of Faith. I became nauseous and feverish almost immediately and he looked over to check my reaction but didn't say anything.

It had been nearly 15 years since I stepped foot into a church. I had nearly vowed never to do so again. Atheism was never considered. I didn't hate God, nor praise Him. We had an understanding.

My mother, everyone called her Kit, was one to sing His

praises, worship and honor Him at all hours of the day — all times of the night. She hummed "thank you Lord" in various pitches during any activity. She made sure we said grace before meals and prayers before bed. She never missed a Sabbath. Those were the memories that I had of her. I last saw her in a church similar to the one at which we had arrived, on her knees singing God's praises with a bleeding heart — in a literal sense.

I was 11, and my mother, as well as two other sisters from Walk of Life Ministries, volunteered to clean the church after each Wednesday night service. It was the only night that the church could be cleaned after service since Fridays and Saturdays were kept holy without labor. Cleaning the church had been a routine for the sisters for as long as I could remember. I was always given the task of cleaning the stained glass windows and the mirrors in the bathroom since only mild vinegar and water solution was used.

One particular Wednesday, the church was packed with visitors from all over to help us begin the celebration of Pastor Anderson's 5-year anniversary. The sermon he preached forced everyone, even the children, to their feet in rejoice for better days to come, for prosperity and peace, and for relief from sickness. The church shouted and praised God. Kit shouted, "Thank you Jesus! Praise the Lord" so excessively that I began to count. I had lost my place around 72.

Trickery

After service, when the parking lots were empty and there was no more shouting and praying, there we were — my mom and I, Sister Denise, and Sister Mattie. We were all exhausted. Sister Denise complained that her feet hurt from standing, stomping, and shouting for so long and Sister Mattie complained that her hands were sore from beating the tambourine. My mother only hummed, "Yes Lord. Yessss Looorrd. Yess Lord," as she handed me the vinegar and water solution and a roll of paper towels.

I was on my way into the bathroom to begin with the mirrors when I noticed gum stuck to the light blue ceramic tile floor. I got on my knees, disappearing behind the pews, and first attempted to remove it with a paper towel. When that attempt failed, lying flat on my stomach on the floor, I started to scrape it off with my fingernail. It began to lift. From beneath the pews, I noticed something strange. There were three pairs of shoes in the building that I had never noticed before, especially at that hour, and they were moving fast, coming closer to where I was lying. Still on my belly, I turned my head left to the front of the church where my mom had been collecting church fans and bibles from the first row. Her toes were pointed toward me, but her feet were not moving. Perhaps she had noticed too, yet she said nothing.

Within seconds, screams rang out in the building as the unfamiliar black boots scattered through the church, one pair making a dash toward the front where my mom had been standing. Another moment later, "BANG!" One of the women was silenced. There were more screams, no prayers. I remained where I was. I couldn't follow the other shoes, but watched as the one who sprinted towards my mother interlocked his legs with hers and pinned her to the floor. I could see her. For a moment she struggled, screamed, clawed and kicked. She turned her head violently as she attempted to break his restraint until finally we locked eyes. Everything stopped. She didn't say anything. She just looked at me, eyes wide with a sense of shame and embarrassment — her black, knee-length skirt was pulled up near her chest, her panties were ripped and lying on the floor next to her. Her body pulsated on the floor for some time. I cried in silence for fear I would be discovered. I didn't break eye contact with her.

He stopped. I could only see his feet again. I wanted him to turn around and run out of the church the way he had run in, leave my mother alone — leave her there so that I could go and help her up from the floor and make sure that she was alright. He didn't. "BANG!" My mother's chest jumped off of the floor as if her heart was attempting to break free from the sternum. Her eyes were still fixed on me. Her body flattened against the cold, hard floor then it appeared as though she fell asleep. "BANG!" The third woman's screams ceased. The church was silent. The unfamiliar shoes were gone.

"I used to come to this church when I was younger," James said, interrupting my thought. He unfastened his seatbelt then leaned over to attain the bible in the compartment behind the passenger seat. "This is the bible my mom gave me when I was 18." He flipped through its pages.

"You know, I'm not really feeling up to this today, James." He looked puzzled, staring me up and down as though I was the devil in disguise, fearing the church house. "I mean, had I known we were coming here, I would have worn a longer skirt or a better blouse. My hair makes me look like a slut, and —"

"You're fine, Taj." He pressed the release on my seatbelt, and without speaking any further, opened his car door and stepped out. I followed hesitantly, fidgeting with the straps of my handbag.

The church was small in size and in number of participants. The entire congregation was gathered around the altar when we walked in. The space was dimly lit. The church was divided in two; four pews were on each side, all unoccupied at that moment. It was warm; the ceiling fans were doing a poor job cooling off the room. We took a seat in the back of the church near a woman in a wheelchair who reeked of cigarettes and alcohol. James went down on his knees from his seat and began to utter words I could not discern.

The devotion leaders were in the front of the room humming harmoniously while men and women cried and shouted praises. The woman in the wheelchair, with her blank countenance, stared off into space, unmoved by any activity taking place within the church. I couldn't say the same. At the thought of Kelvin I was overtaken with emotion. Teary-eyed and saddened, I looked down at James, still on his knees. There was a break in the chanting and I sniffled. It caught James' attention and he looked up almost immediately with a blank expression. I attempted to dry my face, but my condition worsened as I tried to wipe away the guilt of that moment. He stood and pulled me up by the hand. We embraced. He cried. Perhaps the first time I had ever seen him so overcome with emotion that was unfortunately for the wrong reasons.

Trickery

Chapter Twenty-Three

Trickery

A week later James attended a conference in Tennessee and I was left alone in the house. I went through my typical routine; I awoke by 8 a.m., made myself some breakfast, got in a good workout, then spent the rest of the day in front of the television watching re-runs of several shows on BET. One particular morning, I must have pushed myself too hard during my workout because I became nauseated soon after. I jumped into a hot shower hoping it would relieve me, but it didn't work.

San called and asked if I could meet her for lunch and conversation about an issue with which I could only assist her. I was reluctant at first, but considering that James was out of town and San had kept quiet about our ordeal, I figured I had nothing to lose. I agreed to meet her at a café downtown, a central location, in mid-afternoon.

As I dressed for the day, the nausea failed to subside. Then, this feeling as though someone had punched and kicked me throughout my abdomen area began to overpower me, and caused me lie on the bedroom floor for an instant, unable to make it to the bed. After a while, the pain went away. What did I eat? I picked myself up from the floor and continued to dress: beginning with a layer of baby lotion and body spray, then a black Chanel cocktail dress and Ferragamo pumps. I pinned my hair up tightly and added a hint of Dolce & Gabbana perfume behind my ears.

The pain came back to me en route to the location. I pulled over to the side of the freeway and tears began to stream, an irrepressible reaction to the pain. My hands began to tremble while gripping the steering wheel. The need for fresh air was imperative. I drove to the closest exit, pulled over into a gas station, stepped out and circled the car. My legs buckled beneath me and I could feel myself on the verge of fainting. I rested my back against the passenger side tire, not caring that I was sitting on the ground and pressing against a filthy Michelin tire in an eight-hundred dollar dress.

"Ma'am. Are you okay over here?" a male voice spoke, but I didn't see a face. "Can I call someone for you?"

"No. I mean, yes. Please." I stared off into passing traffic, confused about what was ailing me. I wanted to lay my head on the pavement, knowing that I was unable to rise and get into the car. "Please hand me the phone from the front seat." For an instant I considered that the keys were still in the Mercedes' ignition and he could have easily driven away, but I didn't budge.

Trickery

"Thank you," I said, as he handed over the phone and kneeled down to my level, looking me over to determine the issue. He was a white male, perhaps 32 or 33, and fairly handsome. "Thank you again."

"I don't want to just leave you here. Can I ask what the problem is?"

"I don't know. I just don't feel too well. I'm gonna call someone to come and get me."

"Well, I'll wait around until someone gets here. You shouldn't be out here alone like this."

The only person I knew to call was San. She answered on the first ring.

"Don't tell me you're standing me up. I'm not taking 'no' for an answer." She laughed.

"San, I don't feel well."

"Hell, me neither. I'm cramping and I have a headache, but I'm not complaining." I could hear the sound of wind in the background as though she were already in her car.

"No, I was on my way, but I pulled over. I need you to come here and get me. Please."

"Where are you?" She sounded concerned.

At that moment, I began to see two of everything. My vision became blurred and I could feel my temperature rising. I didn't have the strength to hold the cell phone to my ear, so I lowered it to my lap and the generous patron picked it up and began to speak with her for me.

"Hello," he said, "she's going out. I'm calling an ambulance for her." There was silence. "Well how far are you?" Silence again. "We're off exit 214. You're not far. Take the next exit and turn left. You'll see us out here." He placed the phone back into my lap.

"She's on the way," he said. He opened a bottle of water he had purchased inside the convenience store and offered me a drink. The sip offered a slight bit of rejuvenation.

San pulled in moments later and rushed from her car.

"Girl, why are you on the ground? Come on, get up."

"I can't. I feel dizzy when I stand — like I'm gonna pass out or something." I said faintly.

"I got you. I'll help you into my car. Grab my hand." I couldn't lift my head high enough to see her, but her sweet fragrance occupied the air around me.

"Ma'am, I can pick her up and lay her in the back of your SUV — that's if you don't mind Ma'am."

"No, I don't mind," I said, offering my hand to him. "Thank you."

As he lifted me from the ground, San rushed over to the driver's side and removed the keys from the ignition. I heard the alarm chirping, signaling that the doors had been locked. I fit comfortably in the back of San's Escalade, which still had the new car scent.

"So, which hospital do you prefer?" she asked, fastening her seatbelt and looking over the seat at me.

"Whichever is the closest," I said in agony.

"You don't want that. I'm taking you to Baptist Medical Center. They're usually the best when it comes to ER situations." She paused for a moment. "Well, what's bothering you?"

"I don't know. I'm nauseated, dizzy, and there is a pain that's shooting through my entire abdomen. I don't know what the hell it is."

"Well, what did you eat? Any shellfish or red meat lately? Chicken?" She asked, fishing for an explanation.

Trickery

"No, nothing out of the usual. I haven't eaten at all today."

"Hmm. Well, if you ask me, it sounds like your appendix. If that's the case, they'll want to operate on you today. That is a very dangerous organ to deal with. It can explode and possibly kill you."

She scared me with her appendix talk, and I wondered why I believed her of all people.

Once we arrived in the ER, they pumped me for a urine sample and seven vials of blood and, not long after, slowly escorted me into a room, even before others who were there before me. I thanked San for taking me to the hospital, but asked if she could wait in the lobby. Besides, we weren't friends, and her nose was already too much into my business.

My assigned room was small. There was only enough space for two or three people to stand at any given time. The registration staff came in to inquire about insurance and financial matters, then the nurse peeped in to check my comfort and to inform me that they were waiting for my lab results before I would be seen by the doctor.

I lay on the bed staring at the ceiling, wondering what the hell was wrong with me and fearing surgery if San's assumptions were true.

After a half hour there was a new face in the room.

"Ms. Jenson?" A short, gray-haired woman appeared in the doorway wearing a stethoscope and holding a chart.

"Yeesssss."

"How are you feeling?"

"Like crap. Do you have any answers for me?" I stared at her.

She pressed her hand to my left thigh buried beneath the covers. "Well, your urine sample tells us that you're pregnant." My eyes widened.

"But I'm on my period. I can't be pregnant."

"You are also showing symptoms of someone who is miscarrying or may have an ectopic pregnancy. We won't know for sure until we can get you back there for an ultrasound."

"Wait. What? I don't understand."

"We're going to continue to watch your blood count and let you know for sure."

"So I may have to have surgery is what you're saying?"

"It is likely, if it's a tubal pregnancy. I'll get you over to do the ultrasound as soon as possible." I closed my eyes and exhaled slowly. "Don't worry. The surgery isn't so bad. Just two little incisions."

"Does that mean I won't be able to have children later?"

"No, not necessarily. You'll be fine. You should be able reproduce normally." She picked up the chart from the counter. "I'm going to get you in to see the ultrasound technician, okay?"

"Sure. Thanks."

In an instant I thought of James and how he would react to the news of my illness. Then in another instance, I thought of the ordeal San had put me through and how it could possibly be the cause of my situation. I wondered if the assault would prevent me from ever having children when I'm married. I even wondered if James would be willing to stay with someone incapable of reproducing. I rolled back over onto my side and closed my eyes, forcing myself to sleep.

Trickery

Chapter Twenty-Four

When I awoke, San was sitting next to the bed wearing a loose-fitting black dress and a red scarf across her shoulders. Her face was hidden behind her hands and her legs trembled. Her three-inch, basic-black-pumps tapped the floor with each movement.

"What's wrong with you?" I asked.

"No. What's wrong with you? Have they told you anything yet?"

"No. I need to see a different doctor," partially a lie. The staff was in the process of contacting my primary OBGYN to come in and assist me with my condition.

"How long do you think —" just then, interrupting what San was preparing to ask, a female voice interjected from a speaker box above the bed.

"Yes? Did you need something?" she asked impatiently.

"Umm, no, I didn't call you," I responded. "I must have pressed the button by accident." She disconnected without saying anything.

San went on to question me about my comfort level and my health. To tell the truth, she was too concerned for my liking. This was an issue to be discussed by James and me and had absolutely nothing to do with her.

"James should be on the way here by now, so you don't have to stay much longer."

"Okay, that's fine. I just wanted to make sure you were okay." She looked toward the window, then hesitantly at me again. "There was still something I needed to discuss with you."

"YES?" A voice yelled from the speaker box above the bed.

"I didn't call you. There must be something wrong with it." I looked at the button that I was sure I didn't touch. She disconnected again without saying a word.

"They should really get this damn thing fixed and stop giving me attitude." I positioned myself more comfortably on the bed. "What was it that you wanted to discuss?"

"I forgive you." After noticing my discontented expression, she continues, "No, I mean really forgive you – for everything. I've been reading, meditating, praying even, and although I know that I have to forgive you in order to be the woman that I was before I ever met you, I have to confront you first."

What step in her self-help program is this? I thought.

"I knew about Sarai. I knew what happened the night Sarai died." I raised and propped up on the pillow.

"No, let me finish," she continued. "I was angry. You neglected something – someone so important to me – for a couple dollars. I heard the messages Tiki left on your cell phone about what happened that night." She shook her head. "I would have given you that money for the life of my little girl." San stood from her chair in the corner of the room and began to pace the floor on the right side of the bed near the window.

"You know, at first I figured that you were jealous of me – jealous that I was able to get my daughter back. If you would have put in as much effort to get your son as you did into making money with those shows, you would have had him by now. Son?" she chuckled, "what son? You've probably forgotten you had one – so busy living the life." She stopped at the end of the bed and looked directly at me. I listened silently.

"You've always been selfish, and I learned to hate you for it. I couldn't forgive you for what your selfish actions forced me to endure. Hating you took me to a lot of low places. A part of me wanted you to die that night. I was so angry." She pressed the back of her right hand against her mouth, tears filled her eyes.

"There's a lot I want to do with my life, but this can't keep

Trickery

hanging over my head. I realized that my healing wouldn't come from receiving your forgiveness for what I've done to you, but to forgive you for what you've done to me. This has to be the final chapter." She continued to stand at the foot of the bed silently.

I allowed what she'd said to process for a moment before I attempted to speak. I couldn't help but understand her frustration with me after what happened with Sarai, but her attempt to "read me" about my selfishness was a little over the top. I didn't know how to approach the argument. San was more upset than I had ever seen her, even more than the night Sarai died. Her behavior was reminiscent of a grieving mother saying her final words to her child's killer in open court, right before the prisoner is taken away for the last time. This served as her way of healing.

As I made an attempt to speak, the door opened. I couldn't see immediately who was entering, but I could hear footsteps approaching quickly. Without saying a word, James rushed over to the side of the bed and pressed the "CALL END" button on the railing. Had he heard us? Then Seymone appeared, but didn't fully enter the room. She crossed her arms and stared at San for a few moments before turning to leave. "Wait!" San called out to her. Then she disappeared from the room.

153

Trickery

Chapter Twenty-Five

James walked over to the sink and washed his hands. Returning he asked, "How are you feeling?"

I was hesitant about responding, not completely aware of what had just taken place. I answered simply, "I've been better." He lifted my gown and I touched where I told him it hurt as he questioned me about my symptoms, preparing to make his own diagnosis. There was no point in attempting to explain what other doctors had told me. I figured he would better understand their findings and then inform me.

Within 10 minutes Dr. McIntyre entered the room. "Hi. You must be Mr. Jenson."

"No. I'm Dr. James Carter, Ms. Jenson's fiancé."

"Oh, I see," she said, possibly shocked by a handsome black man with such credentials. "Well, how are you feeling?"

"I'm still in pain, but I really just want to know what needs to be done so that I can get out of here."

"Can you tell me what's going on with her, doctor?"

"Well, an ultrasound shows that she is pregnant, but also shows quite a bit of internal bleeding as well. We're still running tests to determine whether or not she is suffering an ectopic pregnancy.

We will monitor her overnight and may have to perform surgery in the morning." She looked at me, and I nodded my head in agreement.

James had backed away from the bed – arms folded. He stared at my midsection, then the floor. At first he didn't say a word. Then, "So you're saying she's pregnant?"

"Yes, her urine and blood tests prove it." She paused a moment. "I am sorry. Was this a planned pregnancy?"

"No, it wasn't," I said.

"So, there's no possibility of her keeping this baby?" James asked.

"Almost none. I'll give you two a moment. I will come back in to check on you in a few hours."

"Thank you," James and I said simultaneously.

He stood with his back pressed against the wall, arms folded and staring at the floor. "James, it's gonna be alright."

"Umm." He cleared his throat. "I think I need some air."

"I want you to stay." I reached my hand out for him but he ignored it and excused himself from the room.

Trickery

I spent hours rummaging through all the thoughts in my mind: from San's comments, to wondering whether or not we were heard, and then to the baby and James' reaction to the idea of losing it. Nurses had come to take me to another room where I would be kept overnight. I called and paged James for hours, but I received no response. I never expected for him to be as upset about the situation as he was. Perhaps he secretly wanted to be a father, or for me to mother his child, but it was nothing that we had discussed openly.

I laid in silence for hours sorting through all of my thoughts until I fell asleep around 3:00 a.m.

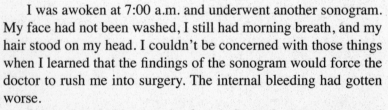

Chapter Twenty-Six

Trickery

I was awoken at 7:00 a.m. and underwent another sonogram. My face had not been washed, I still had morning breath, and my hair stood on my head. I couldn't be concerned with those things when I learned that the findings of the sonogram would force the doctor to rush me into surgery. The internal bleeding had gotten worse.

James was nowhere to be found. Several nurses attempted to make contact with him, but there was never any response. I understood how devastating the situation might have been for him, but he hadn't considered how difficult and physically painful it was for me. I simply wanted him to be there.

A few vials of blood were drawn again and I was prepped for my anesthesia. And it seemed that in the blink of an eye the surgery was over. I awoke as a nurse was wheeling me into the recovery area. As I became more conscious of my surroundings, the pain became more noticeable. Someone had set a small fire in my navel that was spreading throughout my abdomen. I also noticed that no one else was there.

"Nurse." She came over immediately. "Have you heard from my fiancé?"

"No ma'am. I couldn't get him – only voicemail. How's the pain?"

"Can I get something for it? It's really bad."

In addition to painkillers, the nurse handed over my belongings, the clothing that I wore the day before as well as two prescriptions. She offered to call James again, but I asked if she could call a taxi instead. I dressed slowly, preparing to go home, and was wheeled to the front of the hospital where the driver waited.

The taxi ride was dreadfully painful. My wounds had been glued, not stitched, so I feared my incisions would be reopened with each bump and pothole.

Pulling up to the house, I noticed Melinda's Lexus parked in the driveway. My mind moved far quicker than my body did exiting the taxi. Hunched over and slowly stepping one foot in front of the other, I made my way to the front door and let myself in. James and Melinda were sitting in the family room – an open bottle of cognac sat on the table in front of them. They both turned to look at me, hunched over, hair in need of combing and without makeup.

Trickery

"What is this?" I asked. "What the hell is going on? Why didn't you answer my calls, James?"

"You really need to calm down, Taj." He stood.

"What? Is this bitch the reason you didn't show up at the hospital when I've been calling you all morning?" I asked, walking over to her. He seemed surprised by my language.

"This is not a good time," he responded. I was puzzled.

"I think I'll go," Melinda interjected.

"No, stay. You're my friend. Please, just excuse us for a minute – just a minute."

She walked into the office and closed the door. "Have a seat, Taj." James sat back down on the sofa and poured a drink.

"I don't want to sit. I want to know what the hell is going on. What did I do so wrong to deserve this treatment?"

Agitated he said, "I know about you and Santina, Seymone's friend. I know now how you wound up in the hospital over a year ago. I know the type of lifestyle you used to live. So it's obvious that what I don't know now – is you." He took a sip of his drink.

"But tell me Taj, and your honesty is extremely important, what man are you cheating with?" He turned his head to look at me.

"What? I just got out of surgery, you're here with this bitch, and I get the third-degree? This makes absolutely no sense to me, James." I believed Melinda had beaten me to it.

"You better answer the damn question. And I mean honestly," he said, staring directly at me.

"I haven't cheated on you, James." Not an inch of me was willing to confess to him, not in that condition.

He placed his glass down on the table and walked into the kitchen. He reappeared holding a yellow legal pad and a pen. "Here." He shoved it near my face.

"What's this for?" I slowly removed it from his hand.

"I need you to write down a forwarding address." Standing, he reached down for his drink. "I will pack your things and send them there."

"This is ridiculous. Why don't you trust me?" I pleaded.

"Oh, and your son – I almost forgot about that part." He smiled, shook his head, and took a sip of his drink.

"Okay, I know. I had secrets. But they're out now. I didn't want you to judge me. Is that what this is about? We can get past this. I'm still the same person. What can I do?" I continued my plea.

"You can start by writing your new address on that sheet of paper. Then you can get out my house."

Trickery

"Wait, is this about the baby? I don't know what happened, James. It was beyond my control. I can't be the one to blame for what happened."

"Ding! Ding! Ding! Partially right! Where you're wrong is that you think I gave a damn about that baby. It wasn't mine to begin with." He took another sip.

"That's not fair, James. And don't you think you can sit there and treat me like I'm the only one with a past! You never mentioned why your ex-wife left, your history with Melinda is more than questionable. Maybe I didn't trust you with everything, but you could have opened up to me. Saying that it's not yours is just really low."

"I had a vasectomy six years ago. I can't have children." He crushed on a piece of ice that he had taken from the glass then stretched his arms across the length of the sofa. "Perhaps you also learned something new about me. As for the rest, you don't even deserve to ask." He didn't say another word. Any other lie I would tell would be in vain. So I was quiet and did as I was told.

Chapter Twenty-Seven

I packed a few items that I could carry in my condition: a toothbrush, a change of clothes, and some underwear. I called for a cab, and sure enough, the driver who'd dropped me off returned to pick me up again. My thoughts shifted from James. I was focused on survival. I didn't know where I would sleep that night or where my next meal would come from or how I would make another dollar. I figured I could count on one person to be there for me, so that's where I went.

A bit of commotion came from inside San's apartment as my fist lightly pounded on the door. I held on to the door's frame, keeping my balance and realizing that I hadn't taken any medication for the pain that was becoming worse by the minute.

"Can I help you?" Seymone opened the door slightly, but I could see San sitting Indian-style on the sofa with her face buried in her hands.

"Can I talk to San, please?" I pressed against my abdomen and grit my teeth.

"No, there's nothing that you need to say to any of us." News had traveled quickly.

"San, I know you hear me. Please. I need your help." I

attempted to yell. San continued to sit there. "I have nowhere else to go. I need this one favor, please."

"You heard me. Get away from our door." Seymone slammed the door, almost catching my fingers.

"YOU OWE ME SAN! YOU GOT THAT, BITCH! YOU OWE ME!"

"Go to hell!" Seymone retorted from behind the door.

I took the elevator and stumbled into the lobby. From the window I noticed a pharmacy across the street and managed to make it all the way there without collapsing. The 20-minute wait for my prescriptions seemed more like a two hours. Elderly men and women stared as I was balled up in a fetal position and stretched over three chairs in the waiting area. I took the medication and sat there until the pain was manageable.

There wasn't a moment for me to stop and think about what had occurred – how reckless I'd been. What was in front of me was most important. I picked up my small sack of belongings and walked out to the pay phone in front of the store. It had been a while since I'd used one. There was only one person left to call. And I knew that if I had a good proposition, she would come through. So I picked up the receiver and dialed her last known number and almost immediately she answered.

"Hello? Tiki? Is that you?"

Clouds formed overhead and the sun became lost behind them. I knew that soon it would be dark.

Trickery

♛ Triple Crown Publications

Order Form

P.O. Box 247378   Columbus, OH 43224

Name	
Address	
City	
State	Zipcode

QTY	TITLES	PRICE
	A Down Chick	$15.00
	A Hood Legend	$15.00
	A Hustler's Son	$15.00
	A Hustler's Wife	$15.00
	A Project Chick	$15.00
	Always a Queen	$15.00
	Amongst Thieves	$15.00
	Baby Girl Pt. 1	$15.00
	Baby Girl Pt. 2	$15.00
	Betrayed	$15.00
	Bitch	$15.00
	Bitch Reloaded	$15.00
	Black	$15.00
	Black and Ugly	$15.00
	Blinded	$15.00
	Cash Money	$15.00

Shipping & Handling
1 - 3 Books $5.00
4 - 9 Books $9.00
$1.95 for each add'l book

Total $_____

Forms of accepted payment: Postage Stamps, Personal or Institutional Checks & Money Orders. All mail in orders take 5-7 business days to be delivered.

♕ Triple Crown Publications

Order Form

P.O. Box 247378   Columbus, OH 43224

Name	
Address	
City	
State	Zipcode

QTY	TITLES	PRICE
	Chances	$15.00
	Chyna Black	$15.00
	Contagious	$15.00
	Crack Head	$15.00
	Crack Head II	$15.00
	Cream	$15.00
	Cut Throat	$15.00
	Dangerous	$15.00
	Dime Piece	$15.00
	Dirty Red	$15.00
	Dirty South	$15.00
	Diva	$15.00
	Dollar Bill	$15.00
	Ecstasy	$15.00
	Flip Side of the Game	$15.00
	For the Strength of You	$15.00

Shipping & Handling
1 - 3 Books $5.00
4 - 9 Books $9.00
$1.95 for each add'l book

Total $_____

Forms of accepted payment: Postage Stamps, Personal or Institutional Checks & Money Orders. All mail in orders take 5-7 business days to be delivered.

♛ Triple Crown Publications

Order Form
P.O. Box 247378   Columbus, OH 43224

Name	
Address	
City	
State	Zipcode

QTY	TITLES	PRICE
	Forever A Queen	$15.00
	Game Over	$15.00
	Gangsta	$15.00
	Grimey	$15.00
	Hold U Down	$15.00
	Hood Rats	$15.00
	Hoodwinked	$15.00
	How to Succeed in the Publishing Game	$15.00
	Ice	$15.00
	Imagine This	$15.00
	In Cahootz	$15.00
	Innocent	$15.00
	Karma Pt. 1	$15.00
	Karma Pt. 2	$15.00
	Keisha	$15.00
	Larceny	$15.00

Shipping & Handling
1 - 3 Books $5.00
4 - 9 Books $9.00
$1.95 for each add'l book

Total $_____

Forms of accepted payment: Postage Stamps, Personal or Institutional Checks &
Money Orders. All mail in orders take 5-7 business days to be delivered.

♛ Triple Crown Publications

Order Form

P.O. Box 247378   Columbus, OH 43224

Name	
Address	
City	
State	Zipcode

QTY	TITLES	PRICE
	Let That Be the Reason	$15.00
	Life	$15.00
	Love & Loyalty	$15.00
	Me & My Boyfriend	$15.00
	Menage's Way	$15.00
	Mina's Joint	$15.00
	Mistress of the Game	$15.00
	Queen	$15.00
	Rage Times Fury	$15.00
	Road Dawgz	$15.00
	Sheisty	$15.00
	Stacy	$15.00
	Stained Cotton	$15.00
	Still Dirty	$15.00
	Still Sheisty	$15.00
	Street Love	$15.00

Shipping & Handling
1 - 3 Books $5.00
4 - 9 Books $9.00
$1.95 for each add'l book

Total $_____

Forms of accepted payment: Postage Stamps, Personal or Institutional Checks &
Money Orders. All mail in orders take 5-7 business days to be delivered.

♛ Triple Crown Publications

Order Form

P.O. Box 247378 Columbus, OH 43224

Name	
Address	
City	
State	Zipcode

QTY	TITLES	PRICE
	Sunshine & Rain	$15.00
	The Bitch is Back	$15.00
	The Game	$15.00
	The Pink Palace	$15.00
	The Set Up	$15.00
	The Reason Why	$15.00
	Torn	$15.00
	Vixen Icon	$15.00
	Whore	$15.00

Shipping & Handling
1 - 3 Books $5.00
4 - 9 Books $9.00
$1.95 for each add'l book

Total $_____

Forms of accepted payment: Postage Stamps, Personal or Institutional Checks &
Money Orders. All mail in orders take 5-7 business days to be delivered.

♛ Triple Crown Publications

Order Form

P.O. Box 247378   Columbus, OH 43224

Name	
Address	
City	
State	Zipcode

QTY	TITLES	PRICE
	A Down Chick	$15.00
	A Hood Legend	$15.00
	A Hustler's Son	$15.00
	A Hustler's Wife	$15.00
	A Project Chick	$15.00
	Always a Queen	$15.00
	Amongst Thieves	$15.00
	Baby Girl Pt. 1	$15.00
	Baby Girl Pt. 2	$15.00
	Betrayed	$15.00
	Bitch	$15.00
	Bitch Reloaded	$15.00
	Black	$15.00
	Black and Ugly	$15.00
	Blinded	$15.00
	Cash Money	$15.00

Shipping & Handling
1 - 3 Books $5.00
4 - 9 Books $9.00
$1.95 for each add'l book

Total $_____

♔ Triple Crown Publications

Order Form
P.O. Box 247378   Columbus, OH 43224

Name	
Address	
City	
State	Zipcode

QTY	TITLES	PRICE
	Chances	$15.00
	Chyna Black	$15.00
	Contagious	$15.00
	Crack Head	$15.00
	Crack Head II	$15.00
	Cream	$15.00
	Cut Throat	$15.00
	Dangerous	$15.00
	Dime Piece	$15.00
	Dirty Red	$15.00
	Dirty South	$15.00
	Diva	$15.00
	Dollar Bill	$15.00
	Ecstasy	$15.00
	Flip Side of the Game	$15.00
	For the Strength of You	$15.00

Shipping & Handling
1 - 3 Books $5.00
4 - 9 Books $9.00
$1.95 for each add'l book

Total $_____

♛ Triple Crown Publications

Order Form

P.O. Box 247378   Columbus, OH 43224

Name	
Address	
City	
State	Zipcode

QTY	TITLES	PRICE
	Forever A Queen	$15.00
	Game Over	$15.00
	Gangsta	$15.00
	Grimey	$15.00
	Hold U Down	$15.00
	Hood Rats	$15.00
	Hoodwinked	$15.00
	How to Succeed in the Publishing Game	$15.00
	Ice	$15.00
	Imagine This	$15.00
	In Cahootz	$15.00
	Innocent	$15.00
	Karma Pt. 1	$15.00
	Karma Pt. 2	$15.00
	Keisha	$15.00
	Larceny	$15.00

Shipping & Handling
1 - 3 Books $5.00
4 - 9 Books $9.00
$1.95 for each add'l book

Total $_____

Forms of accepted payment: Postage Stamps, Personal or Institutional Checks &
Money Orders. All mail in orders take 5-7 business days to be delivered.

♚ Triple Crown Publications

Order Form

P.O. Box 247378   Columbus, OH 43224

Name	
Address	
City	
State	Zipcode

QTY	TITLES	PRICE
	Let That Be the Reason	$15.00
	Life	$15.00
	Love & Loyalty	$15.00
	Me & My Boyfriend	$15.00
	Menage's Way	$15.00
	Mina's Joint	$15.00
	Mistress of the Game	$15.00
	Queen	$15.00
	Rage Times Fury	$15.00
	Road Dawgz	$15.00
	Sheisty	$15.00
	Stacy	$15.00
	Stained Cotton	$15.00
	Still Dirty	$15.00
	Still Sheisty	$15.00
	Street Love	$15.00

Shipping & Handling
1 - 3 Books $5.00
4 - 9 Books $9.00
$1.95 for each add'l book

Total $_____

Forms of accepted payment: Postage Stamps, Personal or Institutional Checks &
Money Orders. All mail in orders take 5-7 business days to be delivered.

♕ Triple Crown Publications

Order Form
P.O. Box 247378   Columbus, OH 43224

Name	
Address	
City	
State	Zipcode

QTY	TITLES	PRICE
	Sunshine & Rain	$15.00
	The Bitch is Back	$15.00
	The Game	$15.00
	The Pink Palace	$15.00
	The Set Up	$15.00
	The Reason Why	$15.00
	Torn	$15.00
	Vixen Icon	$15.00
	Whore	$15.00

Shipping & Handling
1 - 3 Books $5.00
4 - 9 Books $9.00
$1.95 for each add'l book

Total $_____

Forms of accepted payment: Postage Stamps, Personal or Institutional Checks &
Money Orders. All mail in orders take 5-7 business days to be delivered.